'What do anything?'

Will said harsh unselfish in selling this land for reasons that I'm not prepared to divulge—and I *do* care, because I'm closely involved in it! Whatever happens, the money has to be raised!'

Kathy stared at him. 'So, you're colluding with him, are you?' she said coldly. 'I might have known. Like uncle, like nephew— milking the land for money...'

Judy Campbell is from Cheshire. As a teenager she spent a great year at high school in Oregon, USA as an exchange student. She has worked in a variety of jobs, including teaching young children, being a secretary and running a small family business. Her husband comes from a medical family and one of their three grown-up children is a GP. Any spare time—when she's not writing romantic fiction—is spent playing golf, especially in the Highlands of Scotland.

Recent titles by the same author:

A FAMILY TO CARE FOR

JUMPING TO CONCLUSIONS

BY
JUDY CAMPBELL

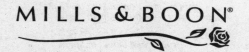

MILLS & BOON®

All the characters in this book have no existence outside the imagination of the author, and have no relation whatsoever to anyone bearing the same name or names. They are not even distantly inspired by any individual known or unknown to the author, and all the incidents are pure invention.

First published in Great Britain 2000
Harlequin Mills & Boon Limited,
Eton House, 18-24 Paradise Road, Richmond, Surrey TW9 1SR

© Judy Campbell 2000

ISBN 0 263 82257 5

Set in Times Roman 10½ on 12 pt.
03-0009-50330

Printed and bound in Spain
by Litografía Rosés, S.A., Barcelona

CHAPTER ONE

'I JUST don't *believe* this!' Kathy Macdowell's voice rose several decibels as she stared at the note in her hand. 'The one person I did *not* want to work with in the whole world, and Harry Lord has to employ him! Why the hell should we have to have such a…a monster in the practice?'

She screwed the note into a ball, and flung it savagely across the room towards the waste-paper basket.

Lindy Macdowell grinned impishly at her sister. 'What's the matter with this person—got two heads, has he?'

'Look,' explained Kathy, with exaggerated patience, 'we're talking about a Dr William Curtis, who just happens to be the nephew of Sir Randolph Curtis—and you know what I think of *him*. He's an arrogant and selfish liar who breaks his promises. From what I know of that family, it's all tarred with the same brush—so William Curtis probably *is* a monster!'

Lindy shifted a piece of chewing gum from one side of her mouth to the other and shrugged her shoulders. 'So, what's the problem—you won't have to see this man much, will you? I mean, doesn't he see his patients and you see yours, and never the twain shall meet?'

Kathy gazed at the teenager in amused exasperation—if only running a practice were that simple!

'For your information, my dear sister, it's a *partner-*

ship practice, you know—we aren't separate entities. It's very important we get on together.'

She thought of all the meetings about patients, decisions in the running of the place, and gave a hollow laugh—she had about as much chance of getting on with a Curtis as flying to the moon!

Lindy squinted into the kitchen mirror and began drawing a thick black line round her eyes.

'So why haven't you told Harry that this guy isn't up to the job? If he knows how you feel perhaps he'll get someone else.'

Kathy sighed heavily. 'That's just the *point*, don't you see? This man's evidently very competent. He's been working in Zimbabwe and had to do all kinds of procedures—his references are impeccable. But,' she added darkly, 'he's probably as overbearing and intolerant as his uncle. I really don't want any involvement in that family. If it weren't for the fact that everyone we've seen up till now has been totally unsuitable, and we need someone desperately…'

'Well, there you are, then—he sounds OK to me,' said Lindy cheerfully, scraping her hair into a band and spreading it over the top of her head so that it looked like a pineapple. 'Beggars can't be choosers, can they? Harry's got to have sick leave, and you can't manage the practice all by yourself—you were on a call when he interviewed this guy, weren't you, so you've never actually met him?'

'Well, no, but I told Harry that I couldn't abide the Curtis family—then he damn well goes ahead and takes him on! But it's no good having a row with poor old Harry about it now. He's jittery enough about his by-pass operation—I don't want to add to the stress.'

With an impatient gesture Kathy flicked back a

strand of honey-coloured hair from her face, picked up a mug from the draining-board and began drying it furiously. There was a crack as the handle broke away.

'Hey—cool it,' murmured Lindy. Gently she took the mug from Kathy's hands. 'Perhaps you're just jumping the gun a bit. How do you know you'll dislike this man, anyway? He might not be anything like old Sir Randolph—perhaps he's a gentle pussycat sort of a person, dedicated to the welfare of his patients.'

Kathy snorted and gave a humourless laugh. 'Don't give me that! I've never met one member of that family who's a gentle pussycat sort of person. They all do precisely what they please, and don't care who they hurt in the process—think they can ride roughshod over anyone less powerful than they are. They're bullies. If our cousin could lease those fields from Randolph Curtis he'd be able to increase his yield one hundred per cent, but, no, that bloody man wants to turn the land into some horrible holiday and leisure complex. Talk about greed!'

She shivered, and bit her lip. She knew all too well about powerful men, didn't she? Men who wanted their own way, who dominated and controlled—men like Randolph Curtis.

She clenched her fists against her sides. She mustn't think of that now—that was all in the past.

She gazed moodily out of the kitchen window at the rolling hills in the distance and the patchwork of stone walls that ran across them. She couldn't bear the thought of that beauty being violated, the delicate balance of the soft meadows and the contrast of the bleak upland moors being lost for ever.

Having carefully applied a startling purple lipstick to her lips, Lindy pulled on shoes with three-inch soles and heels as thick as surgical boots. She grabbed a bag and sauntered to the back door.

'See you later, Kathy. Don't get your knickers in a twist over this man. Remember, old Sir Randolph isn't *all* bad—and he does pay me to look after his horses at the weekends and after school. Sometimes he's quite a generous old stick—gives me some extra money and lets me ride his best horse. Perhaps his nephew has inherited at least some of his uncle's good traits!'

Kathy watched the diminishing back view of her sister with affection as she strode down the lane towards the town. Talk about a character from *The Rocky Horror Picture Show*! Why should Lindy worry about who was taken on at the practice? She was twelve years younger than Kathy and was into her own vibrant life of discos, sport and, perhaps, a little schoolwork!

It had been hard at first for both of them when their mother had died and Kathy had come back to Bentham to provide a home for Lindy. Now Lindy was sixteen, and very different from the sad little girl of two years ago—and, to be honest, in some ways more sensible, less impetuous than her older sister!

Kathy's eyes flicked to the photo on the cupboard of her mother, with herself and Lindy laughing on either side. Her mother had a wistful expression. Whenever she looked at that image of her mother, Kathy felt a knot of hatred squeeze inside her at the thought of Randolph Curtis.

A whining noise from the doorway attracted Kathy's attention and she grinned as she saw a mournful canine face pressed against the glass door to the sitting room.

'Rafter—poor old boy. I've not been thinking about you at all, have I? She opened the door and bent down to stroke the shaggy young dog who looked pleadingly

up at her. 'OK, you're on! I could do with a breath of
fresh air, too—try and put this William Curtis thing out
of my mind. It'll do us both good!'

As soon as she picked up the lead, Rafter flung himself against her joyously, springing up and down like
a yo-yo, his whole being alight with excitement at the
thought of the walk.

Bliss! Early evening in late spring. Kathy lifted her
head and breathed in the balmy air that still had a slight
bite in it. There was a rough path which she and Rafter
took that led quickly into the fields from the last of the
sprawling houses at the edge of Bentham, and here she
let Rafter off the lead. He took off like a rocket, in vain
pursuit of rabbits towards the canal that wandered
through the countryside and formed the boundary of
Sir Randolph Curtis's estate.

Gradually, annoying thoughts about her new colleague receded to the back of Kathy's head. Lindy was
right—as long as he could do the job, perhaps she
could just maintain a professional distance and not allow this Curtis man to get to her. It would be difficult
to accept him—her past experiences could not help but
colour the present, but she'd just have to grit her teeth.
The practice needed help desperately—she couldn't run
it by herself.

Rafter seemed to have disappeared over the brow of
a hill, but she could hear him barking hysterically. Typical mad dog—had probably seen a rabbit and chased
it down a hole. The barking got louder, and all at once
Rafter appeared again, hotly pursued by a small Border
terrier snapping angrily at the bigger dog's heels.

Kathy gave a gurgle of laughter—talk about David
and Goliath!

'You big soft thing!' she chided Rafter as he flung

himself at her like a terrified child. 'Can't you even deal with a little fella like that?' She turned to the irascible little dog. 'Now, shoo! Off you go, you little terror!'

The small dog redoubled its frantic barking, and suddenly she was aware of an athletic figure appearing over the brow of the hill. He was covering the ground with impressive speed, considering the slope, his rangy figure dressed in faded khaki shorts that revealed muscular, tanned legs. A commanding deep voice rang out.

'Magnus! Magnus! Here at *once*—d'you hear me, you wretched animal?'

The Border terrier reluctantly came to a halt, and stood there with a slightly cowed look as he watched his master stride towards them.

'You crazy hound!' The man bent down and tousled the dog's sandy coat, then turned towards Kathy. She found herself looking into the clearest blue eyes she'd ever seen—bright blue like periwinkles, she thought, her eyes locking with his for a second. Thick dark hair, just slightly too long, flopped over his brow. It was an open face, but the firm chin and mouth revealed a certain stubbornness.

The intensity of his gaze seemed to take in everything about her, his eyes sweeping over her tall figure and resting assessingly on her face. Without warning Kathy felt the hairs on her neck prickle under that scrutiny, suddenly only too aware that her T-shirt was a bit too tight, showing off curves that left nothing to the imagination!

God, but this man was gorgeous! She bent down to pat Rafter and conceal the tell-tale blush over her cheeks. Hunky-looking six-foot-tall men were thin on the ground in Bentham, and quite frankly this guy was doing things to her insides that hadn't happened for a long time!

'Sorry about that unprovoked attack!' White, even teeth flashed a devastating smile in the tanned face, making Kathy's legs weaken for a second. 'Hope we didn't startle you or your dog. This bloody creature has absolutely no idea how to behave or to obey anything I tell him!'

The eyes twinkled at her again and a wry grin lit his face. 'Been trying to train him, but it's an uphill job, I'm afraid! He came from a dogs' home, and I don't know about his previous life at all!'

He turned again to the small dog, now lying on the grass and panting, looking with adoring eyes at his master.

'Stay, Magnus!' he said sternly. This seemed to electrify Magnus, and he immediately jumped up and hurled himself on the man's tanned legs. 'See? He has no idea! I'll have to find a dog training centre and enrol us both.'

Kathy eventually found her voice. 'There is one—a training class, I mean—on the high-school playing field on a Sunday afternoon, I think. Do you know the area?'

'I use to know it when I was young—came to stay here with my relatives in the school holidays. Had a wonderful time. It's a great place for young boys to do things—riding, climbing, fishing.'

He grinned at her, looking very boyish himself, and Kathy thought what an easy charm he had—a happy mixture of reliability and strength mixed with humour. He was a stranger, but somehow she felt as safe and relaxed in his presence as if she had known him forever.

'I love the countryside around here, too,' she said simply. 'I just hope it stays this way, that's all.'

They fell into step together along the canal, and she flicked a quick glance at the tall figure by her side and swallowed. Pierce Brosnan, eat your heart out!

'Er…have you just come for a quick visit, then?' She wished her voice didn't sound quite so hoarse.

'No, I'll be here for some time, I think—a few family problems to sort out.'

'Oh, I see. You still have family round here, then?'

The man's expression darkened somewhat, and Kathy bit her lip, cross with herself for seeming so inquisitive.

'I'm sorry,' she murmured. 'I didn't mean to pry…'

Bright aqua eyes smiled at her reassuringly. 'Not at all. It's my father… He's not been too well, and I wanted to be near him.'

'Of course. It must be worrying for you. I hope it's nothing serious?'

'No… I think he'll be all right, but it's good to be here now, instead of thousands of miles away.' He paused for a second, then changed the subject briskly. 'You mentioned that you hoped the countryside would stay the way it is. What did you mean by that?'

Kathy stopped and looked back down into the valley, for they had climbed quite a way up the hill by this time. Bentham stretched below them, a sprawling market town, busy and bustling, with all the problems of a large urban development but blessedly close to the open countryside.

'If you can believe it,' said Kathy slowly, 'there's a move afoot to ruin this lovely place by having, of all things, a ghastly holiday and leisure centre.' She almost spat the last words out, then turned to the man with some passion and demanded, 'Can you imagine the insensitivity of anyone even dreaming that that would be a good thing? I can hardly bear to think about it and, quite frankly, I'm sure it's motivated by nothing but greed.'

'How do you mean?' The man was looking at her intently, at the angry flush of colour on her cheeks and the way emotion had darkened her emerald eyes.

Up here it wasn't cold, but the wind was blowing strongly and Kathy's hair was whipping round her face. She put up a hand to restrain it, and he watched as she struggled to pin it back behind her ears.

'It's far too thick for that,' he murmured. 'I should plait it!' Then his expression changed and he frowned. 'You don't want this...development, then?'

'Of course not!'

'Have you tried to stop it?'

'Huh!' Kathy's voice was bitter. 'Sir Randolph Curtis, who owns the land, also seems to own a lot of people's souls round here. If he wants something he nearly always gets it—bully that he is—and, of course, there are a lot of new jobs involved. There's been plenty of unemployment in this area since the mills closed, and some people positively welcome the scheme!'

'So there might be some merit in it after all, do you think?'

Kathy sighed and shrugged her shoulders. 'I suppose if I were out of work I would be glad of a job anywhere—but once the countryside's gone it's gone for ever, isn't it? Perhaps I'm more worked up because it does affect my family personally.'

The man looked at her sharply. 'How personally?'

Kathy suddenly felt slightly embarrassed. Her side

of the story was beginning to sound rather selfish, as if the main reason was the personal one, whereas it wasn't, really—the reasons were bound up together.

She smiled faintly, aware of the intense scrutiny of his startlingly blue eyes.

'Oh, it doesn't matter,' she murmured. 'Suffice it to say that it's our bad luck that the land should be owned by such an arrogant bonehead as Randolph Curtis!'

'Difficult man, is he, then?' The blue eyes danced at her.

'I can't stand the sight of him,' said Kathy simply. 'Frankly, the whole family takes after him. Think they own the place.'

'You know them well, then?'

He looked quizzically at her and Kathy felt slightly defensive—she didn't know why. Was there the faintest of mocking tones in the man's voice, as if he felt she was making a mountain out of a molehill?

She bit her lip. Perhaps she was beginning to sound slightly paranoid! 'Of course, I don't know *all* his family,' she allowed, 'but the ones I've met have given me the strong impression that they think they own the world!'

The man smiled wryly and shrugged. 'Takes all sorts,' he remarked lightly. He held out a strong, tanned hand, grasping hers, and Kathy gave an involuntary little gasp at the strength of his grip.

'Perhaps I should introduce myself. My name's Will, and at the moment I'm living on the canal.'

He pointed towards the ribbon of water, glinting in the evening sun, and Kathy could see a barge moored by the side of the path.

'You live on a barge?' she said with delight. 'That must be fun.'

'It's a little cramped for someone of my size,' he said ruefully. 'I keep banging my head on the ceiling, and the bunk bed's a mite too short. A friend lent it to me until I find somewhere more permanent. I don't want to be too far out, lovely though it is round here.'

Kathy wondered what this Will did—he could be a fitness instructor or a professional rugby player. Her imagination ran riot. Perhaps he was a film star... Perhaps, and most likely, he had a wife and two children waiting to join him in England.

'If you're going to work in Bentham there are some nice mews cottages which have been done up at the edge of the town. Mind you, they are rather small if you have a family.'

'No, I haven't got that responsibility yet, and I'm unlikely to have it at the present time, I'm relieved to say.'

For some unknown reason, Kathy felt a mixture of relief and disappointment. Relief at him being unattached, disappointment that he didn't want to be attached!

She spoke hurriedly, trying to disguise the rather obvious probing. 'I know there's one for rent there, and they're very convenient.'

She didn't like to add that she actually lived in one of them—she was just helping the man, wasn't she? And her own prospects, she added with a private wry giggle.

As they came towards a stile in the stone wall, they could hear a murmur of voices floating across to them from the next field. Kathy guessed they were walkers, finishing an afternoon's rambling over the hills. She sighed. Come the summer, every weekend would see streams of people enjoying the countryside, and if this new scheme was approved, there'd be thousands more.

The stile was rather a tall, complicated one to prevent deer from getting through, and round the base it had been trampled into a muddy bog. There was absolutely no way she could negotiate her way over, without sinking up to her knees. Recent rain had made it quite treacherous.

Kathy looked at the thick mud ruefully. 'Damn, I should have worn my boots. I forgot about this stile.'

'Perhaps I can help…'

Before she could catch her breath, Will's hands were round her waist and he had lifted her bodily over the mud and onto the top rung. She felt a crackle like an electric shock run through her body at the unexpected strength of his touch, the helplessness of her own body emphasised by the power in his. She gave a little shriek of surprise, and he looked up at her with twinkling eyes.

'Just trying to stop you having a mud bath.'

She sprang down to the other side of the stile, hoping to hide her discomfiture. 'I'm quite capable of negotiating a stile, you know. I've been doing it for years,' she said stiffly.

He had taken her unawares, and his proximity was just too disturbing. She flicked a glance at his face, but he seemed completely unabashed at her change in tone.

With his long legs he managed to clear the marshy ground fairly easily. He jumped down behind her, then pointed to the far side of the field. A group of people was clustered round something on the ground, and there was a general air of agitation. Some of them began waving at Will and Kathy, and one of them started to run towards them.

'I don't think it's quite the happy party it sounded,' he remarked, as a tall, thin man wearing walking boots and jeans panted up, looking distressed.

'Excuse me, but do you know this area?' he said breathlessly. 'We're just finishing our walk and one of our party needs medical help. Do you know of anywhere we could telephone for help around here?'

Kathy sighed, inwardly cursing the fact that even though she wasn't on call, it looked like she'd have to deal with a medical emergency. She wasn't in the mood to feel compassionate. It was probably a wrenched ankle or something similar, she thought irritably. Walkers could be the most careless people! And also, a little voice murmured inside her, she was just getting to know the most attractive man she'd met in ages and needed no interruptions!

With an inward sigh she disguised her impatience.

'By coincidence it so happens I'm a doctor,' she said soothingly. 'Perhaps I could look at your friend and assess the situation.'

The worried-looking man looked as if a ton weight had fallen from his shoulders.

'Thank God for that! We just didn't know what to do for the best! What luck that you happened to be walking near!'

He ran back to the small crowd, and called out, 'It's OK, everyone, we're in luck—this lady's a doctor!'

Kathy pushed through the worried onlookers and said authoritatively to a girl kneeling by the victim, 'Perhaps I could just have a look at this gentleman? See what the damage is…'

There was a visible lightening of the hushed atmosphere around the prone figure and people moved back obligingly.

The girl looked up gratefully. 'Oh, what a relief! We were just getting a bit agitated. Gareth here seems to be in a bit of trouble—says his heart's going like the clappers.'

Kathy looked at the middle-aged man lying on the ground—rather pale, thin and frightened-looking. She bent down and took his wrist, feeling the pulse. It was certainly racing, about 250 beats per minute, she estimated, but in a regular pattern. She smiled reassuringly at him.

'Don't worry,' she murmured. 'I think it will slow down soon.'

Gently she stroked the carotid artery in the man's neck, and gradually there was a slowing down to a more normal rhythm. Colour began to appear in the man's cheeks, and he started to breathe deeply.

'Have you had this before?' she asked.

The man nodded. 'About a month ago—right out of the blue. But I'm very fit, you know. I run a lot, go to the gym.'

'Did you go and see anyone about it? Here, let's see if we can't sit you up a little—make your breathing easier.' Kathy pulled a nearby rucksack under the man's shoulder, propping him up gently.

'The doctor said it was fib—fibber—'

'Fibrillation?' said a deep voice near Kathy. She looked round with a start. Will was squatting next to her. 'Are you in any pain—in your chest or arms?'

The man shook his head. 'No, it just started hammering away without warning, and I didn't seem able to get my breath, felt rather dizzy. It feels a bit easier now.'

Will nodded. 'You're certainly looking better—colour's improving, isn't it?' he said, looking at Kathy.

Kathy gazed at him, slightly taken aback. Surely this Will was overstepping the mark? She'd made it clear she was the doctor. However gorgeous, wasn't he being a bit cheeky, giving his unsolicited and amateur opinion?

'His heart is certainly settling back into rhythm,' she said coldly. She turned back to the patient rather pointedly. 'I think you'll feel much better after a short rest, but it's best that you go and have a check-up at our local hospital here. They'll probably give you an ECG to check this atrial fibrillation.'

'Absolutely!' put in Will. 'This fluttering of the heart can be very frightening, even though it can appear in perfectly healthy individuals. However, best to be sure.'

Kathy stared at Will in angry astonishment. Who did he think he was, muscling in on her territory?

'I'm glad you agree!' Her voice had a cut of sarcasm in it. 'Perhaps you'd go down to the town and ring for an ambulance. I'll stay with Gareth.'

'I can do better than that.' He grinned. He reached into his shorts pocket and took out a mobile phone. 'This is something you walkers might think about taking next time!'

They watched as the ambulance bore Gareth and his friend away to the hospital, and the rest of the walkers straggled down the hill, where apparently they had parked their cars.

'So you're a doctor—a GP?' Will's eyes flickered over her with interest.

'Yes,' said Kathy tersely, still slightly put out at what she deemed Will's unwarranted interference. 'You seem quite interested in medical things yourself.

Have you taken a St John Ambulance course or something?'

Will looked slightly abashed. 'I didn't mean to interfere,' he murmured.

He looked as if he was about to say something else when the sound of a clock striking floated up the valley. Kathy glanced at her watch.

'Seven o'clock!' she gasped. 'I've got to go. A million things to do before going to a meeting. It's been nice meeting you!'

She tried to sound nonchalant, matter-of-fact, but she couldn't help giving a last lingering look at Will's rangy figure and the amazing eyes with laughter dancing in their depths—as if he knew perfectly well what she was thinking!

His glance locked with hers for one heart-stopping second. 'See you around, Doctor,' he murmured. 'Perhaps we'll meet each other again...'

He stood and watched her retreating figure for some time, then murmured to himself, 'With any luck...'

He whistled to his dog and followed the path back down the hill.

Kathy's heart was hammering as she reached the house. She felt cross—cross with the walkers for holding her up, and cross with herself for not finding out more about Will. If she'd had any sense she would have offered to give him supper, perhaps pointed out the mews house opposite that was for rent...

She caught a glance of her gloomy face in the mirror, and laughed. How schoolgirlish could you get? Mooning over a man she'd only met for half an hour. He'd probably have run a mile from her advances, and anyway, she told herself severely, he might not have a family, but a man like that probably had a girlfriend—hundreds of them!

You're a fool, Kathy Macdowell, she chided herself. Picking a man up on a walk and imagining that you've fallen for him—how pathetic! You'll never see him again, anyway!

CHAPTER TWO

FOR the hundredth time, Kathy lightly grazed her wing mirror on the tree that grew far too close to her parking space. Damn! She really must do something about having the lines moved along so that there was more room to manoeuvre—another thing that she and Harry hadn't got round to doing!

There were a lot of things that needed to be attended to, she thought ruefully, flicking a critical glance over the old building that was the Bentham Medical Centre, with its peeling paint and overgrown little patch of lawn. It was situated in a rather run-down area of the old mill town, but the terraced houses that surrounded it were gradually being bought by young people who were doing them up, and only a few of the older residents remained. She suddenly wondered how the place would look in the eyes of this new partner—it certainly could do with a make-over.

Kathy sighed. While Harry, her senior partner, had been ill for the last few months, she had been virtually running the non-medical side of the practice herself. Any spare time had been spent catching up with paperwork or trying to follow her own pursuits. Some time soon, she thought optimistically, she'd get round to doing improvements to the building.

The car park was already full—an indication of a typical Monday morning and a waiting room stuffed with patients! A dog gave a sharp bark at her from a car window, its little face pressed eagerly against the glass. Kathy glanced at it with slight irritation.

'Quiet, you!' she growled at it. Then she smiled. It reminded her of Magnus, the dog she'd encountered with Will. An improbable name for a small dog, she thought with amusement. A picture flashed into her mind of a tall man with long, muscular legs and a pair of devastating blue eyes—he'd certainly brightened up her weekend! Perhaps she was being foolish—it had been so long since romance had featured in her life—but surely she hadn't imagined that special frisson between them? Perhaps she'd take another walk by the canal one day...

Kathy nodded and smiled at the waiting room in general as she threaded her way through toddlers and elderly patients making their way to seats. She looked happier than she felt—her impending meeting with her new partner hung over her head like the sword of Damocles. Would she be able to set aside her dislike of his family to work with him?

She dumped a few files on the desk in the office behind Reception and groaned when she saw the teetering pile of mail in front of her—the paperwork in a practice seemed to take as much time as the patients did!

She glanced across at Ruth, the practice receptionist, whose dour expression augured a difficult morning for everyone in the building. Ruth had a pessimistic disposition and her moods tended to spill over and affect the world around her.

'I'm expecting our new partner, Dr Curtis, this morning, Ruth. Would you bring him in to see me when he arrives? I want to get started immediately on my surgery—it looks pretty full.'

Ruth looked at her balefully. 'He's here already,' she informed Kathy heavily. 'I thought he was a patient and told him to wait his turn—so many people turn up without an appointment—and I said he wouldn't be seen till after ten o'clock.' She gave an angry sniff. 'I wasn't keen on his manner at all. He was rather rude. Said he certainly wouldn't wait an hour—he'd come here to work, not hang around! I hope it's not a fore-taste of what's to come,' she added grimly.

It probably is, thought Kathy gloomily. It sounded as if her fears regarding Dr Curtis were to be fulfilled, although, to be fair, Ruth did get a lot of people's backs up with her lack of tact. Kathy had been meaning to speak to her about that as well, and she couldn't see a Curtis putting up with it for long!

'He's waiting in your room,' said Ruth, nodding in that direction. 'I suppose that means you'll be wanting some coffee?'

Kathy pushed the door of her room open rather ap-prehensively. Was she about to find a younger edition of Randolph Curtis waiting for her?

A tall figure stood by the window, holding the slats of the venetian blind to one side so that he had a view of the terraced houses that lined each side of the road. Dark hair, a little too long, framed the collar of his shirt, and he wore a well-cut dark suit.

Kathy gave a discreet cough, and the man dropped the blind and turned round slowly. Periwinkle blue eyes set in a tanned, open face stared into hers.

Seconds passed as they gaped at each other in dis-belief, then a slow smile spread over the man's face.

'Small world!' he remarked softly. 'I didn't think I'd see you again quite so soon after our walk…'

His glance swept over her tailored navy trouser suit,

and he grinned as he looked at her hair, now firmly anchored in a neat pleat.

'I see you took my advice and plaited your hair,' he murmured.

'What?' Kathy said in confusion, clutching the chair in front of the desk as she stared at him.

'It's…it's *you*,' she finally gasped. 'I mean, you're the man who lives in the barge—Will!'

Her heart gave a disturbing lurch as a broad grin spread over his good-looking face. How in heaven's name had this devastating man turned out to be her new partner? Perhaps he'd come to the wrong place!

'You *are* the doctor who's come to take Harry Lord's place, then?' Her emerald eyes were wide with astonishment.

'At your service, ma'am—William Curtis MD!' He gave a little nod and held out a strong hand. 'I guess you must be Dr Kathy Macdowell, Harry Lord's partner?'

Kathy shook William Curtis's hand numbly. How could this man be any relative of Randolph Curtis? Where his uncle was thick-set, burly and dour, Will had an open countenance and was tall, well set up and good-looking. But, more than that, he had charm and charisma—no way in the world would she have dreamed the two were related!

'Then…then you are Sir Randolph's nephew?'

She felt her face redden as she remembered the conversation she and William Curtis had had when they'd met. Choice words describing his uncle as a 'bully', 'greedy' and an 'arrogant bonehead' echoed in her head with embarrassing fervour!

She swallowed nervously and brushed a piece of hair

from her eyes. He was probably thinking of those re-marks as well!

Then she straightened her shoulders. What of it? Just because this man had turned out to be Dr William Curtis, and her new partner, it didn't change anything, did it? He was part of that arrogant, landowning breed, and his damned uncle was still going to go ahead if he could with his horrible plans. And didn't she still hold Randolph Curtis responsible for contributing to her family's unhappiness in the past? Her new medical partner could think what he liked of her. She didn't care—did she?

She was aware of quizzical eyes searching hers.

'You don't have a problem with him being my uncle, I hope? I seem to remember he isn't exactly top of your visiting list!'

A blush suffused Kathy's cheeks. 'I find it difficult to come to terms with what he's planning,' she mur-mured. 'You probably see him differently.'

Will nodded. 'I respect him very much—he's always been most generous to me. He does have set views, of course—he was never one to sit on the fence—but I often find that he's proved right in the end.'

Kathy smiled weakly. She could hardly tell Will that because of his uncle he was the last person she had wanted to work with! She waved him to a seat and went briskly round to the front of the desk.

'Do sit down,' she said crisply. 'I'm sorry we didn't meet when Dr Lord interviewed you. As he probably told you, we're a medium-sized practice but things have been a little hectic recently. He hasn't been well and, of course, is having bypass surgery this week.'

'And you've been bearing the brunt of it?' Will Curtis looked at her keenly. 'Doing the on-call duty at night as well?' His glance swept assessingly over her face, noting the circles under her eyes, the tense lines round her mouth.

Kathy's pulse quickened as she felt the strength of his scrutiny, but she said lightly, 'We do have an arrangement with a larger practice at the other end of town, and we usually only do two nights out of seven. We cover quite a lot of the town and residential area, as well as the countryside to the west.'

He probably thinks this is pretty dull stuff compared to his work overseas, she reflected, and he's only come home because of his father's illness. Kathy had always loved general practice and never found it boring—the variety of patients, seeing them through their illnesses, hopefully to happy conclusions, and being involved in their lives.

'This may be quite different to your previous work, but we are very much committed to community medicine,' she explained. 'In that respect it may have something in common with what you've been doing. We have a surgery at our local hospital after working hours, one evening a week for emergency cases—or meant to be! Perhaps too many people use it as a useful facility after work, but it does work well, and we've the added bonus of X-ray units close at hand.'

'Sounds good to me!' His mobile face was enthusiastic. 'I take it we only deal with our patients?'

'And those of the other two practices who have surgeries on other evenings. I rather like it, feel I'm keeping in touch with the hospital as well.'

'That's right. Sometimes being stuck at a medical centre can be isolating—I'm all for spreading oneself around a bit!'

He gave his devastating grin, and Kathy reflected

that he was even more disturbingly attractive in formal attire than when she'd first met him. The tan of his face showed up in contrast to his crisp white shirt and his broad frame was accentuated by the tailored suit.

She gave herself a mental shake. This man was a Curtis, for heaven's sake! She was obviously going to have to revise her first flattering impression of him made when she'd met him on the walk. As a colleague and as a Curtis, he was to be kept at a distance, and this stupid initial attraction she felt for him had to be suppressed!

'I believe you've been working in Zimbabwe. Was that in a city practice?' she asked crisply.

Will Curtis gave a chuckle. 'Hardly. It was deep in the veld. I was working for a charity organisation with a special interest in educating the local population in general health care—especially regarding children. But, really, I had to turn my hand to anything—from victims of a lion-mauling to diarrhoea and vomiting.'

She thought of her first glimpse of him the other day in old khaki shorts and shirt, striding up the hill, and couldn't help smiling. It was easy to picture him in the African bush.

'Your experience will probably make anything we can throw at you here quite simple,' she remarked.

He shook his head. 'I hope I'd never be arrogant enough to think I knew everything about medicine— although I am *reasonably* interested in the subject!' There was a teasing twinkle in the deep blue eyes.

Kathy looked at him sharply and blushed. Was he referring to her patronising remarks the other day about him possibly having taken a St John Ambulance course? Whatever, she wished he wouldn't look at her like that—it was darned unsettling!

'You should have told me you were a doctor,' she said quietly.

He grinned. 'You seemed to be very capable of dealing with the problem yourself—and I did get the impression that my help might not have been welcomed!'

'That's not true,' Kathy protested, colouring somewhat. 'I thought you were just an enthusiastic amateur—after all, I knew nothing about you except that you'd come to be near your father.'

Will Curtis's expression changed subtly, his face becoming shadowed, and there was a short silence.

'Is he very ill—in a hospital near here?' Kathy prompted gently.

'No, he's not in hospital, but he's…well looked after.'

'That's good.' There was another short silence. 'Is your father in medicine, too?'

'He is…was a solicitor.'

The tone was dismissive and Kathy had the uncomfortable feeling that this was forbidden territory. Perhaps he couldn't bear to talk about his father's illness. She made an effort to change the subject.

'I suppose you've been working in very primitive conditions and it will seem strange, coming back here?'

Will Curtis shook his head. 'Not at all.' He smiled. 'Lagarda has a beautiful building, in perfect condition, built by local people, with rondavels—thatched huts—surrounding it and used as wards for patients. There's nothing shabby about the set-up there! We were miles from any town, of course,' he conceded, 'and though we had running water and electricity, our equipment was certainly basic—but I think you would have found our quarters pretty comfortable.'

Kathy had a sudden image of his tall figure wearing

a bush hat and shorts, standing outside a building in the shade of a verandah, administering to a crowd of women with young children. Everywhere looked neat and swept clean in the dappled sunlight... Suddenly she was acutely conscious of the dilapidated state of the room they were in—the peeling wallpaper near the ceiling and the tatty blind in the window. She felt slightly rebuked.

'Yes,' she murmured, 'this place probably compares badly with Lagarda. I know it needs a lick of paint.'

He shrugged and gave a swift glance round the room. 'Obviously you've had your mind on other things. Perhaps now I'm here it will be easier... It looks as if you haven't had much time to do anything round here.'

That's telling me, thought Kathy with a tinge of resentment. It's as clear as a bell that he thinks he can put everything right! Was this a hint, perhaps, of the Curtis arrogance she knew she'd have to watch for?

She smiled sweetly at him. 'We seem to have staggered on quite well for many years without the building falling down, I'm glad to say. I'm afraid our patients come first in this practice—the building will have to wait for a while!'

'I see,' he murmured. 'Very laudable...'

'We do have a limited budget as well,' she said crisply, to underline her point. That was true, she thought heavily. In a fund-holding practice there was a definite order of priorities when it came to spending money.

There was a loud bang on the door, and Ruth walked in heavily, carrying two cups of coffee.

'I've brought these in,' she said dourly, 'although I

doubt you'll have time to drink them. The waiting room's heaving!'

'That's OK, Ruth, we'll be starting any minute. This is our new partner, Dr Curtis. I'm sure you'll help him as much as you can.'

Kathy spoke more in hope than conviction. If Ruth took a dislike to someone, it was liable to last a long time!

Will Curtis stood up, towering about Ruth's dumpy figure. 'We have met, haven't we, Ruth? Perhaps we got off to a bad start—certainly all my fault as I didn't make it clear to you that I was going to be working here. Naturally, you thought I was a patient!'

Kathy looked at him in surprise—was this a Curtis talking? The ones she'd met certainly never apologised for anything! Even Ruth looked slightly mollified. She took his proffered hand, and as he gave one of his devastating grins she nodded her head reluctantly before she stumped out.

Will watched her go and then turned back towards Kathy.

'It's true that I did wrong-foot her earlier,' he said in a serious tone, 'but if she did think I was a patient, all the more reason for her to be civil. Is she always as crusty as this?'

'She does tend to have a short fuse,' admitted Kathy, then added defensively, 'But she is marvellously efficient in many ways.'

He shrugged and put down his unfinished cup of coffee. 'She just might put off a nervous patient from making a necessary appointment, don't you think? Perhaps a tactful word to her at the right time?'

Kathy looked coldly at him. Wasn't it a bit early for

Dr William Curtis to be voicing his views? She stood up decisively, indicating that their meeting had ended.

'I don't think there's any need to worry about that at the moment, Dr Curtis. As you've seen, we've a lot to get through this morning!'

His glance swept over her tall figure, standing imperiously by her desk, and an amused glint twinkled in the depths of his eyes. He raised his eyebrows slightly and nodded, as if acknowledging her rebuke, then strode out of the room.

Kathy was left with the unsatisfactory feeling that there were a few things he'd like to change at Bentham Medical Centre and he was only too ready to start calling the shots!

It had been a full morning's work and Kathy hadn't had time to draw breath. Just as she was giving a sigh of relief as the last patient left, Ruth knocked at the door.

'Got a last-minute case here, Doctor—Pat Layton's brought in her mother, Mrs Forster. The old lady's had her handbag snatched in the supermarket down the road. They thought it would be quicker to bring her in here than go to the hospital.' Ruth dropped her voice slightly. 'If you ask me, it's her daughter that's more in shock than Mrs Forster—she seems a bit hysterical. Her mother's hand looks bad.'

Kathy sighed. There'd been a lot of petty crime in Bentham recently—broad daylight seemed to be no deterrent. It was too bad when a woman of Mrs Forster's age was subjected to an attack.

She stood at the door and waited for the two women to come forward. A policeman hovered in the background and a little knot of curious onlookers was peering through the door.

Mrs Forster was eighty-three, a tiny woman with a slightly humped back. They certainly chose their victim well, thought Kathy grimly, someone who couldn't possibly put up a fight.

She was slightly surprised when she looked at Pat Layton. She was a tall, smart woman in her mid-fifties, well known for her involvement in community affairs, a magistrate and councillor—the kind of woman who took things on with calm efficiency. Today she was shaking with emotion, a handkerchief pressed to her face as if to suppress her tears. Ruth was right—in comparison, Mrs Forster looked fairly calm.

'Do come in and sit down,' Kathy said, gently putting a comforting arm round Mrs Forster's back. 'I believe your handbag's been snatched—what a horrible experience for you.'

The old lady gave a spirited snort. 'I'd give that young thug a piece of my mind if I caught him—that I would! I'd just got my pension out of the post office, too. They don't want to earn an honest day's wage, that sort!'

Pat Layton suddenly gave a loud sob. 'Oh, Mother! How could they do this to you? You poor thing—it's terrible, terrible!'

Mrs Forster looked scornfully at her daughter. 'Pull yourself together, Pat. Anyone would think it was you who'd had their handbag snatched!'

Kathy made a swift intervention. 'Did he hurt you at all, Mrs Forster? What happened exactly?'

Her voice was low and soothing. She wanted to give the woman a chance to tell the story in her own words, to get it out of her system. However feisty she appeared on the outside, she knew that the old lady was probably deeply shocked by the incident.

For the first time Mrs Forster's voice trembled slightly, revealing the depth of the trauma to her, and she wiped her eye with a shaky hand.

'I…I was just going to get some biscuits off the shelf. The digestives—those are what I like, you know, with tea…'

Kathy waited patiently. All these details would seem an important part of the story to Mrs Forster.

'Then suddenly I felt my shoulder jerk. My handbag strap was over my shoulder, but I was holding onto the bag with my left hand. Whoever it was pulled the bag as hard as he could, so the metal part really cut across my finger and I had to let go.'

She looked fiercely at Kathy, rallying slightly in the telling of the story. 'If I hadn't been taken by surprise I'd have got the young bugger…'

Kathy smiled. There was still plenty of life left in the old girl yet! 'Let me look at your hand, Mrs Forster—is that where it hurts?'

She took the old lady's left hand gently, and turned it palm up, inspecting a purple swelling on the finger above the patient's wedding ring. She looked at it closely. A dribble of blood oozed out, and Kathy realised that in the rough treatment Mrs Forster's ring had cracked, and the two ends had pinched together behind the finger.

'This must be very sore, Mrs Forster. Your circulation's being impeded by your broken wedding ring— that's why your finger's rather blue. We'll have to get the ring off. If you'll just wait here, I'll get our new partner, Dr Curtis, to look at it.'

For the first time Kathy felt a twinge of relief that

Will Curtis was there. In latter weeks Harry had often not been able to come in, or had gone home early. It was comforting to think that she had a reliable back-up at times like these.

Will Curtis was sitting in the office at the back of Reception, writing something down. He looked up as Kathy came in.

'Ah, you've finished, too?' he said. 'I wanted to have a word with you. I've been making a few notes...'

'Can it wait a minute? We've got a slight problem— I'd appreciate your help. I'm a bit stumped as to what to do with an elderly patient who's injured her finger.'

Will stood up quickly. 'No problem. What happened?'

'A youth snatched her handbag in the local super-market, and the metal part of the bag cracked her wedding ring. It's impeding her circulation and the ring needs to come off quickly. Any ideas how to do it?'

He grinned. 'You don't spend two years in the African bush without picking up a few hints. If you've got a wire-cutter somewhere in this building, I think I can do it without taking off the entire finger!'

Will's broad presence in Kathy's surgery seemed to have a calming effect even on Pat Layton, although she stared at the wire-cutters in his hand as if they were a pair of daggers.

'Nothing to worry about,' he said cheerily. 'We'll soon take the pressure off that finger, Mrs Forster.'

He sat in a chair close to the old lady, bent forward over her hand and in no time at all held up the two halves of the wedding ring with an air of triumph.

'Geronimo!' he murmured. 'Nothing to it!'

'I've never had that off since the day I were wed,'

remarked the old lady. 'It's been on my finger for sixty years, and now some young criminal's broke it!'

Will looked at her compassionately and put a gentle hand on her arm. 'It's a wicked shame, Mrs Forster, but at least you can mend your ring—you might have lost your finger!'

His gentle gesture wasn't lost on Kathy. What patient wouldn't have felt soothed by that simple touch? She knew that this man would win the hearts of most of her patients—recently, Harry Lord's illness had made him so testy that some people had refused to see him. Will Curtis would do much to redress the balance.

Will turned to Kathy. 'What do you think about this finger?'

'It looks slightly distorted,' she replied, looking at it critically. 'Better have it X-rayed, and it might need a splint. I think you ought to go to Casualty, Mrs Forster, just to make sure it's not fractured. They'll also make it more comfortable for you. The practice nurse here will dress it for you temporarily, but we've no X-ray equipment.'

Pat got up from her chair, looking rather white. 'I'll take you there right away, Mother—the car's outside.'

'Eh, lass, you're the one that looks as if she needs a doctor, not me!' Mrs Forster stared at her daughter and shook her head. She went out of the room quite jauntily, and said loudly to the two doctors, 'I don't know what's got into the girl—she seems to seize up at the slightest thing. If she'd had anything about her she'd have chased that thief and brought him down!'

Pat bowed her head and scuttled out of the room behind her mother. Kathy watched her exit with a frown. The woman certainly didn't look a bastion of the community now!

'So—anything else I can help you with?' Will's eyes twinkled. 'I quite enjoy minor operations, and I certainly didn't anticipate one like that!'

'Thanks,' said Kathy wryly. 'I don't think I could have done the wire-cutter technique quite as well as you! I must remember to keep some handy for the next mugging!'

'Does a lot of that happen around here, then?'

Kathy shrugged. 'I don't suppose more than any other community. A lot of youths looking for quick money to feed their drug habit probably.'

A sardonic smile passed over Will Curtis's face. 'Perhaps a new injection of jobs in this area would be a good thing, then—give these yobbos something to do.'

Kathy looked at him sharply. Was that a reference to his uncle's holiday and leisure centre plans? An angry flush rose in her cheeks.

'Good for your family, you mean,' she rejoined tersely. 'Is this a plug for your uncle's expansion plans?'

'Possibly,' he said noncommittally. 'But, I assure you, Randolph always goes into things very thoroughly, looking at every side of the question. He's a very thoughtful man.'

Kathy snorted derisively. 'Well, let me tell you, Dr Curtis, your Uncle Randolph, of whom you speak so highly, is deliberately hanging on to land that *my* cousin desperately needs to make his farm viable. Sir Randolph's selfishness is probably going to result in a lot of farm workers losing their jobs!'

Will raised his hands as if in surrender. 'Sorry! Touchy subject!' His eyes swept over her indignant figure, lingering for a microsecond on her flushed cheeks and parted lips, then he said evenly, 'Perhaps you're a little blinkered in your outlook, Dr Macdowell. There's always another side to the coin, isn't there?'

Kathy bit back a swift retort. She didn't want to have a major row on the first morning of Will Curtis's appointment—after all, he *had* turned out to be rather useful so far. Even so, his remarks about his uncle didn't ring true to her. A picture rose in her mind of the day she'd tackled Randolph about his treatment of her own cousin, John. His gruff voice echoed in her ears.

'Your cousin, my dear, has not been a model tenant. I'm not minded to lease him any more land when he can't look after what he has now!'

His dark eyes under their bushy eyebrows had looked at her implacably. 'I am sorry to cause you distress, but perhaps if he limited his intake of alcohol it might help his cause!'

Kathy remembered how she had seethed with anger at his remark. 'John may have had health problems which have been exacerbated by your treatment of him,' she'd flamed, 'but you're just using that as an excuse. You always get your way, don't you? Especially in dealings with my family!'

She recalled the strange look of bitterness that had flashed across Randolph's face, then he had given a slight bow and had observed quietly, 'I'm sorry you think like that, Kathy, but things are not always as simple as they seem…'

'It's as clear as daylight to me,' she'd snapped. 'Your tenants mean very little to you!'

Kathy was brought back to the present by the sound of Will's deep voice.

'I'll do some of the home visits now if you like,' he offered. 'By the way, I noticed that we seem to have quite a few blank appointments—people just not turning up. Does this happen a lot?'

'I can hardly help that,' she replied defensively. 'Patients are sometimes very cavalier.'

'Perhaps we're being too lax with them—could we run a name check and see who consistently misses appointments and write them a letter?'

She snapped green eyes at him. 'I haven't had the luxury of that kind of spare time, Dr Curtis.'

Her cheeks burned angrily—the man had only been here five minutes and he was finding fault! The irritating thing was that he was right. All the things he had mentioned were problems that she had at one time thought about herself but had put to the back of her mind. Perhaps she had grown used to living with them. Could it be that a fresh pair of eyes were regarding them more critically?

He smiled disarmingly at her. 'Might save yourself a lot of time if you made it clear that missed appointments weren't acceptable... By the way, perhaps you could bring yourself to call me Will—I shall certainly call you Kathy out of earshot. After all, we are partners! See you later! *Ciao*, Kathy!'

He raised a hand in salute and for a second his eyes locked with hers. Kathy's heart suddenly missed a beat. Then he swung out of the room, leaving behind an impression of strength and humour.

Kathy stared after him with a confusing mixture of emotions—she hadn't felt that tingle of excitement near a man for such a long time now, and yet she seethed with irritation at his ready criticism. Overriding it all, however, and forcing her heart into overdrive when he was near her, was acute awareness of him as one of the dishiest men she'd ever met!

CHAPTER THREE

LUNCHTIME was like an oasis for Kathy. She usually went back to her house and let Rafter run for fifteen minutes in the garden whilst she had a sandwich and read the paper. The past few days had been different—somehow she felt slightly on edge, and full of restless energy. She needed exercise and remembered ruefully that she'd joined the gym just down the road from the surgery about a year ago and had only seldom visited it.

Was it the appearance of one William Curtis that made her want to tone up and look her best? His presence had made her reassess quite a few things—from the state of the surgery to her own lifestyle!

Whatever, she suddenly had the commendable urge to get fit for summer, and so here she was, power-walking on the treadmill and finding it slightly more difficult than she would have believed! Another ten minutes and she'd have done one and a half miles and would be ready to tackle some weightlifting.

She felt a measure of irritation that it should have taken a meeting with Will Curtis to kick-start her into action, but she had to admit that she was feeling good already, doing something she was always advising her patients to do—take exercise!

Panting through the routine, she looked wryly at her reflection in the full-length mirror opposite her. To be honest, there was some way to go before she'd achieve the fitness she wished for! Brilliant red cheeks, aching limbs and short breath showed that her level of fitness wasn't very good for a young woman merely doing brisk walking. She would have a quick shower and wash her hair, before going back to the surgery for the afternoon. She certainly didn't want Will Curtis to see her looking such a wreck!

Will Curtis! She seemed unable to get the damned man out of her mind. He was completely different from how she'd imagined. He had charm and charisma where she had been expecting arrogance—and yet there was an inner steel there, and she could imagine that if William Curtis wanted something, he got it and brooked no opposition. She couldn't blame him for supporting his uncle's plans and being loyal, but surely he must see what a blight they would be on the countryside?

There was the sudden grind of the machine next to her starting up, and a deep voice cut into her thoughts.

'Ah, I see you're working off your stress levels in the best way possible—I'm impressed!'

Kathy looked up with a start and nearly fell off the treadmill as the object of her thoughts appeared beside her, wearing a rugby top and bottom over knee-length Lycra shorts!

Will Curtis pulled off his ruby top, revealing an impressively tanned muscular torso and arms. Kathy's already high cardiac rate went up a few notches, and she tried to ignore the tingle that knotted her stomach at the proximity of his powerful body.

He started at a jog, soon increasing to a brisk trot, and grinned at her.

'Fifteen minutes should get the adrenalin pumping,' he remarked cheerily, 'then I can catch up with my notes before the evening hospital surgery. Will you be at the centre this afternoon?'

'Yes,' panted Kathy, trying to get the words out smoothly and not give away the fact that she was almost too breathless to speak. 'I have a well-woman clinic this afternoon—nothing too arduous.'

She slowed down her pace a little to catch her breath, and her eyes flicked over to the dial on his treadmill. He had speeded up considerably and was pounding away at a mind-boggling average of nine miles an hour.

'Do you do this most days?' he enquired easily, his long legs setting up a steady, even pace.

'No...not...not often enough,' gasped Kathy raggedly, drawing to a halt and switching off the machine quickly before he could read the dial with her feeble attempt shown on it.

'I'm just going to do a few weights to tone up, then I'll go back when I've showered. See you soon.'

She walked away as briskly as she could, trying to hide her gulping breaths. She didn't want to give Will Curtis the impression that she was horribly unfit!

The owner of the gym was standing by the weights machine. A good friend of hers—they had been at school together and belonged to the same tennis club— Kathy knew it had been Sue's dearest dream to own a gym and had seen how hard she'd worked to make the place viable.

'Hi, Sue, how are things?' she said warmly as she started to lift the lightest of the weights.

Sue Croft smiled a little wanly and shrugged her shoulders. 'So-so. Having a bit of a nightmare at the moment, though...'

'How come?' Kathy looked with concern at her friend's worried face.

Sue sighed heavily. 'I suppose you've heard about this new leisure and holiday centre that's being proposed?'

Kathy nodded and flashed a quick look across at Will Curtis, now pounding away easily without any shortage of breath.

'What about it?' she asked quickly.

'You can guess the effect it will have on this little gym—I'm still paying off the loan I got to fit it out.'

'But it's doing well, isn't it? You always seem pretty full.' Kathy's voice was full of concern—she'd always admired Sue's enterprise in starting the fitness centre.

'Yes,' admitted Sue, 'we started off very well, but people are always on the lookout for bigger and better, and this new centre will doubtless have a swimming pool and more machinery than I could ever hope to get. Already, people are making enquiries about the new place.'

'Oh, Sue, that's really hard—you must be very worried.'

'I am. I'd hoped to go on to bigger things myself but, as it is, I may have to lay off staff—if not close down altogether if this darned thing goes ahead—unless someone can persuade Randolph Curtis otherwise.'

Sue looked very cast down and a surge of anger coursed through Kathy. It was all so unfair. If Sue's gym closed down there'd be a knock-on effect for local traders—a big new centre would probably not use the little man round the corner. She glanced at Will. Surely it would be possible to persuade him to come over to her side and ask his uncle to reconsider?

She lifted herself from the weights machine and put her hand on Sue's arm in a comforting gesture. 'If I can do anything, I will,' she promised. 'It's a crying shame!'

Will was now slowing down on the treadmill. The slightest sheen of perspiration was on his body and he seemed to be breathing remarkably easily. He gave Kathy a friendly nod and she bit her lip. However attractive she found him, she wasn't going to let that deter her from pointing out another casualty of his uncle's plans.

He watched her walking over, his eyes wandering appreciatively over her Lycra-encased body and following the line of a bead of perspiration travelling slowly down her cleavage. Kathy blushed self-consciously under his scrutiny and picked up her towel, wrapping it closely round her defensively.

'You off now?' he remarked. 'You look quite warm—obviously got your cardiac rate up pretty high.'

'My heart's absolutely fine,' she rejoined. 'I'm in good shape, thank you very much.'

'Of course you are,' Will murmured, his eyes dancing. He pulled on his rugby shirt and remarked, 'It's useful, having the gym so near the surgery. We'll probably be the fittest doctors in the district.'

'Well, I hope you make the most of it,' Kathy said curtly. 'It may very well have to close down if your uncle sells his land to a leisure and holiday centre! Sue's put so much effort and money into this project— she couldn't cope with that kind of competition!'

'I think maybe your friend is being unnecessarily gloomy,' said Will lightly. He started to towel his legs briskly and looked up at her under his brows. 'You forget—most of the people who will use that centre will be holidaymakers, not residents. The fees would probably be too high for locals, anyway.'

'I don't think that will calm her fears at all,' rejoined Kathy. 'Look, is there any chance that you could persuade your uncle to back off from this idea? Surely he doesn't need the money—it's just a project to keep him happy and fill the coffers even more, isn't it?'

Will Curtis's expression changed suddenly. The humorous quirk of his mouth vanished, and his eyes hardened to a steely cobalt. He stepped towards her, so close that they were almost touching and she could smell the maleness of him, feel his breath on her cheek. He pierced her with a stony gaze.

'You have absolutely no idea what his reasons are for developing his land this way,' he grated, 'so perhaps you could keep your thoughts to yourself. I think I know my uncle better than you and, believe me, he has my backing *whatever* he wants to do. Furthermore,' he added harshly, 'if I were you I should drop this obsession of yours about the development of the land— it can only harm our working relationship!'

He picked up his towel and strode off without a backward glance. Kathy stared after him with a mixture of embarrassment and anger. Maybe she had overstepped the mark in her criticism of Randolph, but she had certainly seen another side to Will Curtis. When roused, his genial nature vanished very quickly! As for his statement that he knew his uncle better than she did—she would question that. There were things about *that* member of the family that only she knew about!

An unwelcome image suddenly swam before her eyes…the page of a diary in her mother's handwriting, words that accused Sir Randolph of despicable behaviour and revealed a terrible sadness in her mother's life—and all because of that man!

She blinked back the tears that pricked her eyes and

decided that, no, she had definitely not been too hard in her criticism of Randolph Curtis. That man deserved all she could throw at him!

There were still five minutes to go before her clinic, but Kathy was surprised to see a few women waiting outside and peering through the windows of the centre.

'Why don't you go in and wait in Reception?' she asked one of the patients.

'You seem to be having a bit of trouble in there at the moment—and your receptionist wouldn't let us cross the threshold!'

The speaker sounded disgruntled, and Kathy reflected ruefully that Ruth seemed to make a habit of getting on the wrong side of people.

She opened the door and marched in, staring in horror at the reception area she'd left less than an hour earlier. Water was dripping from the trapdoor in the ceiling and already large puddles had formed on the chairs and carpet. Ruth was frantically mopping up what she could and carrying armfuls of files away from the stricken area.

'What on earth's happened?' Kathy gasped. 'Has there been a burst pipe? I can't understand it. It's a warm day, and it's not raining...'

'Goodness knows,' said Ruth gloomily. 'It started just after you went out. I've contacted that plumber fellow you usually get, and he's coming when he can—but, of course, he's got an emergency he's dealing with at the moment, anyway!'

Heaving a sigh of irritation, Kathy flopped down in a chair and rubbed her forehead wearily. If only this hadn't happened now!

Will would be here any minute, and in his present

mood how would he react to a medical centre dripping
with water, a clinic waiting to start and nowhere for
the patients to sit?

She recalled with some embarrassment smugly in-
forming Will that they put patients before buildings at
her practice. Now the irony was that they might not be
able to treat any patients at all without a building to
practise in!

'I always said this would happen,' said Ruth with
dark satisfaction. 'We've had damp patches on that
wall for many a month now. The plaster will probably
start cracking soon if you ask me!'

Kathy bit back the retort that no one was asking her.

'We'll just have to manage as best we can, then,
Ruth. I know it won't be easy—'

'No, it certainly won't—'

'But I'm sure you'll manage!' A deep voice inter-
rupted them, and Will strode over to the desk and
peered up at the ceiling. 'I think I could get up there
and pack a few towels around the cavity in the roof—
that might hold it for a bit. At least I'll be able to see
what's causing it. Would you turn off the water at the
mains, Ruth? It's probably under the sink in the
kitchen.'

He smiled winningly at Ruth and she nodded dourly,
before plodding off to the little kitchen and intoning,
'I was just saying to Dr Kathy that this was a disaster
waiting to happen. We've been promised for months
that something will be done about the building…'

He turned to Kathy and she was relieved to see that
his cold demeanour had melted somewhat. He gave a
wry smile.

'Looks a bit of a mess, doesn't it?'

She nodded dolefully. 'God knows what all this will cost…'

As if reading her thoughts, Will turned and glanced over the room.

'Perhaps this is an opportunity to have a thorough assessment of this building. What happened exactly?'

'It was very sudden—a gush of water out of the blue, apparently. I suppose a pipe must have burst.' Kathy looked rather defiantly at Will. 'Nobody could have foreseen it, you know…'

His amused blue eyes locked with hers for a moment.

'Of course not—you're not clairvoyant! Luckily, I'm your man when it comes to doing emergency surgery until the expert arrives…'

At least, thought Kathy gratefully, he isn't moody. His cold annoyance in the gym had evaporated, and he seemed totally interested in the matter in hand. He leapt onto the reception counter and at full stretch managed to push open the trapdoor in the ceiling. A small waterfall descended on his head and splashed over the floor.

'Damn,' he muttered, then grinned down at her, his black hair now plastered, dripping, to his head. 'Not quite such a good idea perhaps! Pass me up those towels Ruth's brought when I've swung into the loft, would you?'

Kathy and several patients who'd wandered in watched open-mouthed as his lean body swung perilously in the air before he hauled himself through the aperture and his long legs disappeared into the loft after him.

'Wow!' exclaimed one young patient. 'Superman!'

Ruth plodded back into Reception with two buckets

and shook her head lugubriously. 'That looks a dangerous thing to do,' she asserted.

As if on cue there was the sudden sharp crack of splintering timber and a shower of plaster and wood-shavings descended to the floor.

'Blast the bloody thing...' Will's exasperated voice floated down to Reception. 'The boards here have had it. Watch out! I'm coming down again.'

He swung himself down easily enough and stood dusting his hands, then he looked at Kathy with slightly raised eyebrows.

'Perhaps, Dr Macdowell, I could have a quick word with you in your room?'

Kathy followed him meekly into her surgery—her assertion the other day that the centre had lasted very well so far now sounded hollow indeed!

Will closed the door firmly behind them and looked at her with a flash of irritation in his blue eyes. Small drops of water still ran down the side of his face and he brushed back his damp hair with an impatient hand.

'This building is terminally ill,' he said tersely. 'I don't know how long it is since anyone looked in that loft, but even with my amateur eye I can see bare wires. And the flood's been caused by a fractured water tank—it must have been dripping away for ages. We're going to have to spend some money, Kathy, or hold a surgery outside on the grass!'

Kathy bit her lip and nodded. 'I guess you're right. We shouldn't have let it go so long. We did have warning signs, as Ruth said, with damp walls and peeling wallpaper, but somehow in the last few months it hasn't been a priority...'

'Well, then, I suggest you make it a priority and quickly—I'm damned sure I don't want to practise medicine in a building that's likely to fall down round my ears. It seems that things here have been put on the back burner for too long!'

The sting behind his words made Kathy's cheeks redden. It was all very well for him to criticise her management of the practice, but she'd been coping almost by herself for the past months.

She put her hands on her hips and angrily reflected that his remarks were just the sort of thing she might have expected from a Curtis. He seemed to assume that these things were easy to implement in the midst of doing a busy job!

She drew a deep breath. 'I shall make sure you aren't in danger or inconvenienced in any way,' she said coldly. 'I'll have the builders here today.'

He swept a quick look round her room. 'Good idea! I should get the decorators as well,' he remarked briskly.

Kathy felt her blood pressure rising. 'Look, I know the place isn't perfect—'

'I don't want it perfect immediately, just in a workable condition,' he interjected shortly.

He glanced at his watch, then, as if shaking off his irritation, looked Kathy full in the face, his eyes softening as they swept over her worried expression. He gave a wry smile and touched her flushed cheek gently.

'Come on, it's not the end of the world! I'll leave you to put things in hand and I'll start writing up some notes. Perhaps you could let me know how things are going.'

The shock of his gentle touch sent a tingle through Kathy's body and her cheek burned. For a second they were silent as his gaze mingled with hers and a shiver of attraction darted through her like an arrow.

A loud bang on the door made them both start and signalled Ruth's stolid appearance.

'Dr Curtis, I forgot to tell you in all the kerfuffle—there was a phone call for you. They want you to ring back and the number's on your pad. I'm afraid the line was bad, but I think they said it was "W.G."'

In an instant Will Curtis's expression changed...was it agitation or surprise that flitted briefly over his face? Then it vanished, to be replaced by a look of stern composure.

'I'll ring from my room,' he said curtly. 'Please, hold my other calls. I don't want to be disturbed on any account for the next few minutes.'

He turned abruptly on his heel and marched out. Kathy wondered fleetingly why a phone call should so obviously upset Will, then she dismissed the thought and sat down with a baffled sigh.

This man was occupying her thoughts too much, she reflected ruefully. He had shown another facet of his character today. He was definitely not a man to be pushed around, and yet just when she was about to explode with anger at his presumptive manner she would feel her knees go weak as she saw that melting smile. Damn and blast Will Curtis!

Irritably she pushed the button that activated the screen in Reception, showing that she was ready for her first patient.

'I'm sorry to bother you, Doctor. You seem so busy today with the flooding and everything. Is it a bad time?'

Pat Layton's pale face peered round the door rather fearfully as if she was frightened that Kathy would shout at her.

'No...no, Mrs Layton. I'm glad you've come—do sit down. I was going to pop in and see your mother later today. I heard from the hospital that her finger was fractured, poor lady. How is she in herself?'

'She's remarkable,' sighed Pat, shaking her head in disbelief. 'I always knew my mother was a force to be reckoned with, and she's proved it.' She gave a nervous half-laugh. 'I'm afraid I feel very feeble compared to her!'

'I hope they catch the culprit. Did you see him, or were there more than one?'

Pat's face flushed. 'No...no,' she said quickly. 'I didn't really get a proper look at them. There were two of them, and possibly one by the door, but it was difficult to see...'

'Of course—these things happen so quickly, don't they?'

There was a short silence and Kathy looked carefully at the woman before her. Pat Layton had been a patient at the centre for many years, although she'd rarely had to make use of its services. Leading such a busy life, Kathy's knowledge of her was mostly through the local newspaper where photos would appear of Pat opening a new old folks' home or giving her policies regarding council affairs. She always looked supremely confident.

Today it was different—as it had been when she'd come in with her mother. There was a defeated look about her, her normally well-coiffed hair rather disordered, her face pale.

'You didn't come in especially about your mother, did you?' prompted Kathy gently.

Pat bit her lip and clasped her hands together. 'Well...no, Doctor. I... Well, things seem to have been getting on top of me lately. I know it sounds ridiculous, and I can't stand people who moan about nothing, but I feel absolutely exhausted, and things that might not have got me down before really upset me now.'

She looked for a second as if she was going to cry, but she composed herself and gave Kathy a weak smile.

'Stupid, isn't it? I think I just need a tonic or something.'

Kathy leaned forward on the desk and shook her head. 'Of course it's not stupid. You're very wise to come. What sort of things are upsetting you?'

A blank expression froze Pat's face and she said quickly, 'Oh, nothing… Just silly little things, as I said. I seem to allow some worries to assume monumental importance and, of course, they're not important at all—not at all,' she repeated firmly.

'Well, then,' said Kathy, smiling reassuringly at her, 'let's have a look at you.'

She took the woman's hands in hers and looked closely at the fingernails, then turned them over and looked at the palms. Gently she pulled down Pat's eyelids and inspected them. She noticed how pallid they were.

'Have you any other symptoms besides tiredness?'

Pat nodded reluctantly. 'I do feel dizzy sometimes, and my heart pounds—I thought perhaps it was the menopause—and I don't seem to have the appetite I once had.'

'What about your bowels? Have you lost any weight?'

Pat shrugged. 'I don't know about losing weight, but I sometimes get awful indigestion—that certainly puts me off eating.'

Kathy nodded. 'I think I'd just like to feel your tummy—perhaps you'd just slip off your skirt and lie on the couch.'

The woman looked slightly alarmed. 'Do you think I have some stomach disorder, Dr Macdowell? I've never had any trouble before.'

'I just want to get a general picture of your physical condition to start with,' Kathy said soothingly. 'Lie back and relax. You probably aren't used to relaxing with your busy life so make the most of it! Apart from your council work and being a magistrate, you have two sons, don't you? You can't have much time to yourself...'

Kathy was startled at the look of panic that suddenly seemed to cross Pat's face at the mention of her children. Every muscle in her body tensed and her eyes were big and anxious.

'Do you know my sons?' she asked sharply. 'They...they've not been to see you or anything?'

'No,' replied Kathy, baffled by the woman's reactions. 'I don't think I've seen them for a long time. They're teenagers, aren't they? Why? Are you worried about their health?'

'No, no...not at all. They're fine, no problem!' The woman gave a slightly forced laugh. 'Just the usual teenage worries, you know!'

She lay back on the couch and Kathy bent over her, listening carefully through the stethoscope to the bowel sounds. She could hear the rhythmic gurgling of the intestines as they did their work and, by gently palpating the woman's abdomen, she was able to ascertain that there seemed to be no enlargement of her kidneys, spleen or liver. She hooked the stethoscope back round her neck.

'Everything feels and sounds fine,' she said. 'But that's not to say that there isn't an underlying problem.'

'So you don't think I've come unnecessarily?' Pat started to put her skirt back on again. 'I thought I was being fussy.'

'Far from it,' Kathy assured her firmly. 'I want to do a blood count on you, and I'll give you some treatment for the indigestion now. You need to come back next week for the result of the blood test and we'll go from there, depending on the results.' She paused for a second, looking searchingly at Pat's drawn face. 'Is there anything else worrying you? No other problems?'

'Of course not—what else could there be?' Pat got up quickly from the chair and dusted her skirt meticulously, not looking at Kathy.

'Right—then I'll see you next week with your results. Go to the hospital pathology department tomorrow morning with this form and they'll do a blood test.'

'Thank you, Doctor.'

Pat gave Kathy a nervous smile, and walked quickly out of the room. Kathy frowned as she watched her go—she was convinced that the woman hadn't told her the full story. There was something bothering her besides her health, of that she was sure. 'Underlying worries?' she scribbled on the notes to remind her of her suspicions about Pat Layton.

The sound of hammering drew Kathy from her room. Ruth was conferring with a workman and the noise was coming from the cavity in the ceiling. Kathy felt a wave of relief that something was being done about the mess.

'How long do you think this will take to put right, Charlie?' she asked, looking worriedly up at the jagged hole still ejecting odd flakes of plaster and wood chippings.

'Not long,' he said reassuringly. 'I told that new doctor of yours that if we worked this evening it would be perfect by tomorrow—no worries.'

Kathy grinned. Charlie Lennox was as optimistic as Ruth was pessimistic!

'Where is Dr Curtis?' she asked Ruth. 'He's doing the hospital surgery this evening and I wanted to fill him in on a few things before he left.'

'Oh, he swept off in a great rush after his phone call,' replied Ruth. 'Said he had to visit someone urgently, but that he'd be back very soon.'

'So he didn't say where he was going? What about his mobile phone?'

'Not working,' said Ruth.

Kathy felt a prickle of indignation. Suppose she needed him, or there was an urgent patient situation—how the hell was she supposed to contact him?

'I see,' she said, tight-lipped. 'Perhaps you'd tell Dr Curtis to come and see me then when he comes back?'

She marched back to her room, feeling slightly let down. She had imagined that Will would have been more professional than to vanish without a contact number. She'd had enough of coping virtually on her own—she needed someone utterly reliable.

By the end of surgery Kathy's irritation level had risen considerably. An hour had passed, and there was no sign of her new partner. If he didn't come in the next five minutes, she'd jolly well go home and let him go to hell!

Ruth buzzed through on the intercom. 'I've got a call from your sister,' she intoned. 'She's at the stables and sounds a bit flustered—says she wants an urgent word.'

'Put her through, then.' Kathy smiled to herself. Lindy probably wanted to tell her that she'd be back late and wouldn't need any supper. She often went round to one of her friends' homes to do her homework.

'Hi, Lindy. If you want to go to Jenny's, that's OK— I'm out tonight myself. If you do want some supper, there's plenty of salad in the fridge.'

Lindy's voice sounded strained and very young— quite unlike her normal upbeat tones. 'It's not about that, Kathy. We've got a bit of a drama here. It's Sir Randolph…' Her voice sank to a whisper.

'What about him? Has the bloody man been rude to you?'

'No…no. He collapsed in the yard as he was about to go for a ride. He seems in awful pain and he's a horrible colour, but he won't let me call an ambulance. Says he's got to be seen by his nephew, Will. He wants his opinion first!'

To her shame, Kathy felt a lurch of satisfaction. So the efficient Will Curtis had been caught out just when his precious uncle needed him! Then she bit her lip. Poor Lindy! In a frightening situation and no back-up.

'Look,' she said soothingly, 'I can't get Will Curtis right now, but I'll come along and assess the situation myself. Where is the pain—in his chest?'

'No. It…it's in his groin. He's curled up in agony…'

'Try and put the man in a comfortable position and tell him help is coming. With any luck his nephew will be along soon—I'll leave a message for him. And, Lindy—keep calm!'

She leaned back in her chair for a moment, drum-

ming her fingers on the desk. It sounded as if it could
be a strangulated hernia—a real emergency—but if the
stubborn old fool wouldn't let Lindy call an ambulance
then she herself would have to deal with it.

She felt a wave of resentment building up inside her.
This really wasn't good enough—the whole reason for
getting another partner was to back her up, especially
in this sort of situation. Dr William 'Efficient' Curtis
was quick enough to point out faults he saw in the
practice, but he had let her down in the most basic way
possible, by not being available when he was needed.

Kathy stretched forward for a pad and angrily
scrawled a message on it.

'As I was unable to contact you I have gone to see
your uncle myself. Apparently he's been taken ill and
wants you urgently. Please go to his stables as soon as
you can.'

She scribbled her signature and grabbed her medical
bag, rushing out of her room and giving the note to
Ruth.

'Make sure Dr Curtis gets this. I'm on my way to
the Curtis stables now and I hope to see him there,'
she said briskly, marching out of the centre.

My God, she thought angrily as she shot off down
the road from Bentham in her car. She couldn't wait
to put William Curtis straight and tell him exactly what
she thought of his cavalier ways—and he'd better have
a darn good excuse!

CHAPTER FOUR

'I WANT you to try and relax while I just feel the site of your pain. Please, I must try and ascertain what's wrong.'

Kathy was kneeling by the side of Randolph Curtis. The man's body was doubled up with agony and his face was grey. It wasn't the best place to examine a patient, she thought grimly, flicking a quick glance around the stable-yard. Lindy and the housekeeper, Betty Cooper, had done their best and had laid him on a rug with a cushion under his head, but the man was obviously in acute shock, his breathing rapid and shallow, with a weak, thready pulse.

She touched his face. It was cold and clammy, and yet there was a faint sheen of perspiration on his brow.

'Don't touch me,' growled the man. 'It's a bit of muscle strain—don't know what the fuss is about. Just felt a little faint, that's all.'

You obstinate old tyrant, Kathy reflected, taking no notice of his remarks and gently examining his groin. Fancy refusing to let Lindy send for an ambulance until his precious nephew came! Well, he'd have to make do with her at the moment, she thought with a touch of satisfaction.

She looked at Randolph's face as he blanched in agony at her touch.

'I think it's a little more than muscle strain,' she commented wryly.

She delicately probed in the hollow between the

lower abdomen and the top of the thigh, and from the bowel sounds she could hear through her stethoscope she was sure that there was an intestinal blockage.

Lindy had been standing a tactful distance away with Betty Cooper, but as Kathy put away her stethoscope and pulled a blanket over the patient to keep him warm she stepped forward, her anxious young face looking in a frightened way at Randolph.

'What do you think, Kathy?'

Kathy smiled at her sister reassuringly. 'You certainly did the right thing ringing me up,' she said quietly. 'Sir Randolph needs immediate hospitalisation. You mentioned that he'd also been vomiting?'

'I was only a little sick. What a fuss!' Randolph turned restlessly on the rug. 'A painkiller is all I need—an aspirin or something.'

'We'll need to do more for you than that.'

Lindy's eyes widened. 'What's the matter with him, then?' she whispered.

'Stop that damned whispering,' grunted the prone figure before them. 'I think I'm entitled to know as well. For God's sake, what the hell's going on?'

Kathy grinned. Whatever she thought of Randolph Curtis, he certainly had spirit! She didn't like the man, but he was a patient in desperate need of help and reassurance—and he still managed to be as contrary as he could!

She reflected on the irony of the situation. Here she was, trying to do her best for the man she believed had caused her mother such distress. She longed to tell him just what she thought of his selfish plans for the estate, but instead she sighed and knelt down beside him.

'I'm pretty sure you have a strangulated hernia, Sir Randolph, which means a section of bowel has pro-

truded through a weak area in the abdominal wall.
There's no question but that it should be attended to
as soon as possible.'

'What do you mean?' said the man faintly through
clenched teeth. 'Attended to? You attend to it, then!'

'I mean you need an operation to push back that part
of the bowel. I suspect that it's twisted, which is causing the acute pain. If we allow it to stay like that much
longer, the blood supply will be impeded.'

She didn't add that loss of circulation could lead to
gangrenous tissue—perhaps that would have been a bit
brutal.

Randolph Curtis looked stonily at her. 'I don't like
hospitals—never have. Are you sure an operation is the
only option? What about drugs and things?'

'I'm quite sure.' Kathy's voice was firm. 'You must
have immediate surgery.'

Randolph Curtis struggled to raise himself on his
elbow, grimacing with pain as he did so.

'Where's my bloody nephew? I want his opinion before I start being sliced open...'

'I'm afraid I can't tell you,' said Kathy coldly. 'He
had a phone call and I presume he went to an emergency, but he didn't say where. I've left a message for
him at the medical centre to tell him what's happened,
so he may turn up. But we can't wait much longer. I'm
calling an ambulance.'

Lindy gave a little cry. 'There's a car coming up the
drive—this is probably Will now!'

Kathy turned and watched grimly as the car swung
into the stable-yard and screeched to a halt. Better late
than never! Will's tall figure emerged and he strode
over to them, looking slightly dishevelled, his long,
dark hair flopping over his eyes.

Without warning, her heart gave a sudden bound as she saw him and she caught her breath. Every time he was near her or looked at her, he stirred her blood, and despite the irritation she felt for him at the moment his appearance always changed her world for a second. How ironic that she should feel this acute attraction for a man she'd been determined to dislike!

Did he feel anything for her at all? she wondered. He had a fairly laid-back attitude to life, and it was hard to tell if the amused, appreciative glances he gave her were his normal response to an attractive girl or something more special. A few teasing words probably meant nothing at all!

Now she was surprised to notice a disturbed and agitated manner about him. Normally his demeanour was very relaxed and reassuring when he saw a patient. Of course, this wasn't just any patient, Kathy reminded herself, it was his uncle.

However, it seemed to her that Will forced a smile as he dropped down beside Randolph and smoothed the older man's hair from his brow.

'What's going on?' he demanded. 'What have you done to yourself?'

'Where the hell have you been?' whispered Randolph, echoing Kathy's sentiments exactly. 'We've been waiting…' His voice trailed off, and his head dropped back on the cushion Lindy had provided.

Will looked sharply at him, and held his wrist lightly, feeling the man's thready pulse. He turned questioningly to Kathy. 'What do you think?'

'I'm pretty sure he's got a strangulated hernia, with the acute pain he's suffering, and there are over-active bowel sounds, indicating some sort of blockage. The protrusion of the bowel is quite evident.'

Kathy's voice was crisp and unemotional. She would deal with the question of Will's unavailability later.

'Is it irreducible?'

'Yes—and he's been vomiting—but he's very unwilling to let us get him to hospital until you give the nod.'

Will glanced at the patient, now lying with eyes closed. 'He's got no choice,' he said curtly. He pulled out his mobile and punched out some numbers, talking rapidly into the mouthpiece—giving directions to the ambulance on how to get to the scene and an indication of what was wrong with the patient.

'They won't be long,' he muttered. He took his uncle's hand and said gently but firmly, 'You must go to hospital, Randolph—there's no way out.'

'Just give me a slug of whisky,' whispered the man pleadingly. 'That would do the trick…'

'Kill you, more likely,' said Will with a wicked grin.

'But I've never spent a day in a damned hospital in my life. I'll discharge myself as soon as I get there,' Randolph threatened in his weak voice.

'You discharge yourself,' said Will grimly, 'and I won't spell it out to you, but it won't be a hospital you'll be needing…' His voice softened. 'Now, don't be an awkward old beggar—you know how much I need your support at the moment. You must get better so, for my sake, don't make a fuss.'

Kathy wasn't surprised that the bluster left Randolph as he subsided meekly back onto the cushion with a sigh. He was probably feeling so ill that any decision-making was out of the question.

'You're a bully, Will, but as usual I suppose I'll give in. You've enough worries besides me.'

The sick man attempted a smile through the agony

he was feeling, and to her astonishment Kathy felt a flash of admiration for him. There seemed to be a great rapport between uncle and nephew, and she appreciated the teasing but firm way Will dealt with Randolph. They were obviously very fond of each other.

She wondered briefly what Will had meant when he'd said he needed his uncle's support 'at the moment'. It probably referred to the fact that his own father was ill.

Will turned to Lindy. 'Were you here when it happened?' he asked gently.

The distress in the teenager's face was evident. Her mascara-lined eyes had run a little where she'd obviously been crying—a common reaction to a traumatic event. She blew her nose vigorously and looked at him bleakly.

'Yes,' she murmured, her lip trembling slightly. 'I didn't know what to do for the best—your uncle was absolutely adamant he didn't want anyone but you to look after him.'

'You did very well,' he said with an encouraging smile. 'It's a terrific shock when something happens quickly like this. Don't worry about Randolph. Once he's in hospital, he'll be fine. Why don't you go with Betty and your sister to the house and get some tea? I'll stay with my uncle until the ambulance comes. He can eff and blind at me all he likes then!'

Kathy put her arm round Lindy as they walked up towards the rambling house. 'Will's quite right. You've had a shock and a cup of tea will do you a power of good!'

'And a nice sugary biscuit,' declared Betty. 'You need sweet stuff when you've had a shock like this, don't you, Kathy?' She looked back at her employer lying on the ground and shook her head. 'It's a terrible thing. It happened so quickly, and if Lindy hadn't been there I don't know how long he'd have been without help.'

'I was just holding the horse for him,' said Lindy with a tremor in her voice. 'It's that lovely big one, Zephyr, and I'd saddled him up. Just as Randolph had his foot in the stirrup, ready to jump up, he suddenly fell back with this horrible sort of scream, clutching his groin.' She shuddered. 'It made me realise how hopeless I am. I just didn't know what to do, and the horse was prancing about all over the place.'

'You did just fine,' said Kathy, hugging her. 'The hernia had probably been there mildly all the time, but the sudden strain of trying to hoist himself into the saddle could have caused it to push even more through the abdominal wall. And as for not knowing what to do, I tell you if I had to deal with a huge, prancing animal like Zephyr I'd probably have fainted!'

Lindy blew her nose and looked at her sister. 'You know, I really like Will. He's so funny and kind—and he thought about me as well as Randolph. Couldn't you try and like him just a bit?'

Kathy flushed. That was the trouble—she was beginning to like him more than just a bit! The trouble was remembering that she wasn't *supposed* to like him!

She tried to sound casual. 'Now, how have you got to know Will so well? You don't come to the surgery much and you're at school during the week?'

'He comes up to see his uncle, and when I'm at the stables, helping out, I see him then. I know you don't like the Curtises, but they've both been really kind to me—especially Randolph. And as for Will, it's not his fault that Randolph's selling off the land, is it? Anyway, I think there must be a good reason for that—something we don't know about!'

Kathy looked sharply at Lindy. 'Whatever do you mean? He's obviously selling it because he's being offered a good price. Has he told you something about it?'

'No,' admitted Lindy, 'but I'm sure he wouldn't sell it just for profit. He really loves his land—he's told me so!'

Kathy snorted in disbelief, then turned as she heard the sound of the ambulance coming up the drive. She felt a sudden compunction at not seeing her patient into the ambulance, and patted Lindy on the shoulder.

'I think I'd better go back to Will and just see Randolph into the ambulance before returning to the surgery. You go on up to the house with Betty, and I'll make you a real energy-boosting supper tonight. See you later!'

'So how is your uncle?' enquired Kathy. She looked searchingly at Will, who was slumped in his chair in his room at the surgery, his long legs stretched out in front of him. It was late in the afternoon and she was about to go home, but she wanted a word with Will first. She needed to know why he had left so abruptly earlier with no word to anyone as to where he was going.

He ran a distracted hand through the dark hair that frequently tumbled over his eyes. 'His BP was pretty low when he got to Bentham Infirmary—eighty over forty—although the paramedics had put him on a drip. I saw Kevin Stuart, the consultant, and he's going to operate as soon as Randolph's stabilised.'

'I'm sure Randolph will be fine—it's usually a very

successful operation. I think your uncle's a tough old man.'

A twinkle lurked in Will's eye. 'You think so, do you? As far as I can tell, he's too damned tough. He's had discomfort there for weeks apparently, and hasn't done anything about it—typical!'

'I told you he was stubborn. Perhaps you'll believe me now!'

Will shrugged and smiled. 'Ah, as regards everyday life, I think Randolph is tenacious rather than stubborn!'

Kathy felt a flash of irritation—he always seemed to defend the damned man! However, there were other matters she wanted to discuss with her new partner besides his uncle. She drew a deep breath.

'I have to admit I was somewhat annoyed this afternoon,' she began coldly.

Will raised a questioning eyebrow. 'How come? Something to do with the flood in the surgery? They're getting on well with the repairs now.'

Muffled banging could be heard through the surgery walls.

'Not at all,' Kathy snapped. 'More to do with your disappearance halfway through the afternoon with no indication where you'd gone. We also drew a complete blank with your mobile. As you've learnt, we *did* need to find you! I presume you were out on an emergency?'

He stood up slowly and nodded, bunching his fists in his pockets and staring out of the window.

'Something like that,' he said tersely. 'I was called away on urgent business.'

'So it was one of our patients?' persisted Kathy. Why was he being so darned secretive? She and Harry had always discussed their patients with each other—

it was a wise routine that ensured that they had as much background as possible about everything.

He turned and looked at her levelly. 'No, it was to do with my father. I'm sorry you couldn't get hold of me, but I'll make sure it doesn't happen again. The message service seemed to have broken down.'

'Then perhaps next time you go gallivanting off, you'll give us some idea where you are going.'

He frowned and his voice hardened. 'I didn't ''gallivant off'', as you put it. I was contacted and told to come and see my father immediately. And, as I said, I was unable to use the mobile.'

There was a hard, forbidding aura about the man, thought Kathy. Criticism and Will Curtis didn't mix!

She was puzzled. Just what *was* the matter with his father, and why should it be such a mystery. There was only one way to find out!

'Could I ask what's wrong with your father?'

Will's face became shadowed but his voice was softer. 'He...he has a few problems,' he said briefly. 'He'd received news that he had to discuss with me urgently.'

Kathy coloured angrily. 'For heaven's sake, if he wasn't ill surely you could have discussed the matter after this evening's surgery?'

'It wasn't an option, I'm afraid.' His cold tone discouraged further questioning. 'Believe me, it *was* important,' he added with quiet emphasis.

Kathy swallowed hard and flashed a glance at his implacable expression. She really didn't want a huge row so early on in their relationship, but Will's attitude wasn't doing her composure any good! It would have been nice to have had more of an apology but, then, he was a Curtis, wasn't he? It just wasn't in his nature!

Her green eyes sparked angrily at him, and a flush of annoyance spread over her cheeks. Will looked at her for a long moment, then suddenly put out a hand to pull a tendril of hair from her face which had escaped from the neat chignon. Kathy jerked her head back impatiently, and a mischievous smile lit his face.

'You know, you look extraordinarily beautiful when you're angry,' he remarked, folding his arms and gazing at her critically with his head to one side.

'What?' Kathy was totally taken aback. How…how *dared* he change the subject with such a blatantly sexist remark? To her intense horror she felt a slow blush spread over her face. This was ridiculous! Here she was, trying to point out the difficulty he had put her in, and he was turning it into some kind of a joke. And what was more, she was allowing herself to feel flattered in a schoolgirlish way!

She shot him an icy glance. 'I'm sorry,' she said coldly. 'That's the kind of thing pathetic men say when they're losing an argument.'

He raised a sardonic brow. 'I'm sorry you think I'm pathetic,' he remarked easily. 'I've said I'll do my best to ensure it doesn't happen again.'

He paused and looked at her with a slight smile. 'Don't you think you're losing your sense of perspective in this matter? Perhaps you need to broaden your horizons a little—have a few more interests. There is a life outside the surgery, you know!'

Kathy looked at him angrily. 'How *dare* you imply that I'm narrow-minded?' she flashed. 'I have a lot of interests—when I have the time to pursue them, that is. That's why I was hoping my new partner might be more supportive. Perhaps your wider horizons in Africa have made you a little laid-back in your attitudes!'

He was very near her. When he looked down at her she could see dark flecks of green in his blue eyes.

'I'm sorry,' he said gently, putting a conciliatory hand on her arm. 'It's true that things were perhaps a little more relaxed in the bush, compared to Bentham, but I would never want you to feel I was letting you down.'

His open, strong face seemed to have a kind of yearning in it, as if there was more he wanted to say but could not express. Kathy bit her lip. Maybe, she thought suddenly, she *was* treating this whole episode a little too seriously, making a mountain out of a mole-hill. She didn't want to ruin a new working relationship before it had barely begun!

She drew a deep breath. 'Look, I'm not criticising your work—it's just, well, I need the confidence to know I can get hold of you when I need to. Perhaps the last few months have made me run on a shorter fuse than I should...' She looked at him speculatively. 'It must have been quite a culture shock, coming back to England. Perhaps you didn't want to leave Zimbabwe. If your father hadn't needed you, would you have returned?'

Will smiled wryly. 'You're right—I hadn't been planning to come back so soon. I loved Africa and the job—it was hard to leave.' He brushed back the hair from his forehead and leaned against the wall, his eyes regarding her quizzically. 'But I had a very pleasant surprise when I arrived back here. Bentham was as beautiful as I remembered it as a child. I love it...and all it has to offer. I know I shall enjoy life here.'

His eyes held Kathy's for a second and she coloured slightly. 'I have to go now,' she murmured quickly, picking up her briefcase and walking towards the door.

She opened it slightly and then paused, a mischievous smile playing around her lips as she looked back at him.

'As a matter of fact, Will, I *do* have plenty of interests, and they're nothing to do with medicine!'

An amused glint danced in his eyes. 'And what might they be?' he enquired.

'Nothing that you would find of any consequence, but I'm in a play which the Bentham Dramatic Society is putting on. We have a rehearsal tomorrow evening, so don't think there's nothing else in my life!'

The amused glint turned to a broad smile. 'Well, well,' he said softly, 'I should have guessed. You're in amateur dramatics!'

'You might be interested to know,' she said loftily, 'it's to help raise money for a protest against the plans your uncle has to sell his land!' She gave Will a pert glance, and swept out of the room.

Will sat down abruptly as the door closed, and crumpled up a piece of paper savagely in his hand, tossing it inaccurately towards the waste-paper basket. Sometimes, he thought bitterly, he wished he could rewind the scenario of his life so far. He had begun to hate the sound of a phone. Wasn't that how the present mess had started?

He recalled with cinematic clarity the innocuous ringing of the old telephone in the main building at Lagarda Medical Centre in the wilds of Zimbabwe two months ago. He had been sure it would be his father, ringing to wish him well on his birthday. The swishing of the fan in the ceiling had stirred the air round in the dark hut, and children's voices had chattered outside as he'd picked up the phone. He'd had so much to tell his father! How he loved working in the bush, how kind and appreciative the people were…

But it hadn't been the kind of phone call he'd been expecting at all. The clipped tones of his uncle and the unbelievable news he'd given had dashed Will's dreams of spending another year in Zimbabwe, and had made him feel he was living in a nightmare.

And now the phone call this afternoon! He didn't know whether to feel elated or cynical. It was hard, being an only child, he reflected. All the responsibility and decision-making lay on his shoulders and, although Randolph was being an amazing support, he sometimes felt he was totally alone. Perhaps there *was* some light at the end of the tunnel. Having seen his father this afternoon, it appeared that there might, just might, be a resolution to the problem.

He tapped out some numbers on his mobile phone and spoke into the receiver.

'Is that Conrads' Solicitors?' he asked. 'Will Curtis here. Tell Mr Conrad that I'd like to speak to him about the latest development.'

The rehearsal wasn't going too well. To begin with, the leading man wasn't there. He was suffering from a sprained ankle, and Kathy herself was feeling tense after the dramas at work, particularly her altercation with Will the day before.

Why, she wondered angrily, had she allowed that man to get under her skin? She could have mentioned the fact that he should have left a contact number in a calm manner, without getting so wound up. After all, in the end it had turned out all right and he'd arrived at the stables in time. Perhaps, she thought despondently, she *was* losing her sense of humour…too much work and too much time dwelling on the Curtis family!

'Kathy? You should be making your entrance now, dear. This is the important scene, you know, where our hero declares his love for you…'

Molly the producer's voice cut through Kathy's thoughts and she jumped guiltily to her feet.

'Oh, I'm sorry… Can we go through that bit again? I'm afraid I lost my place.'

Molly raised her eyes to heaven and said sadly to the room at large, 'What can I do? The leading lady's in a daze and we haven't even *got* a leading man… All right, everyone, let's just break for a quick cup of tea while I ponder on which scene to do next.'

'This all sounds rather dramatic!' a voice whispered in Kathy's ear. 'Things not going too well, then?'

Kathy whirled round in surprise. Will was standing there in jeans and a battered old lumber jacket, an impish grin on his face! She stared at him in amazement.

'*You!*' she gasped. 'What on earth are you doing here?'

He gave a chuckle. 'The friend I'm leasing the barge from told me they needed people to make scenery here. I like playing around with woodwork so I came along. Of course,' he added softly, 'there was the added incentive of watching you perform. If you hadn't have mentioned it, I might not have come!'

Kathy flushed. She certainly hadn't had it in mind that he should watch her attempts at acting. She could imagine the look in those sardonic eyes as he observed her haughtily rejecting the hero's advances and forgetting her lines at important moments!

'I—I wouldn't have thought a little society like this would have interested you,' she stuttered. 'It—it's all very low-key—and you might be embarrassed about our opposition to your uncle's plans!'

'I'll have to live with it,' he said lightly. 'I know not everyone supports his point of view. As I said before, I think it's important that people should have interests outside their work, and this sounds fun.' He looked down at her smilingly. 'You don't mind me coming, do you?'

Kathy shrugged helplessly. Not mind? Those cobalt eyes, watching her every clumsy move, were about the most inhibiting thing she could think of! She wished like mad that she'd worn more flattering clothes than her old jeans and sweatshirt!

Molly bustled up with a sheaf of scripts in her hand. She looked appreciatively up at Will's tall figure. 'Ah,' she boomed. 'A new recruit? What are you coming to do?'

'I'm Will, and I was told you needed scenery makers and shifters—if so, I'm your man!'

Molly beamed. 'That's absolutely marvellous! Always delighted to have new blood!' She paused for a second and looked at him assessingly. 'You wouldn't do anything else, would you? We are a bit short of people tonight.'

Will raised an eyebrow. 'Like what?'

A feeling of dread suddenly swept through Kathy. No! Surely Molly wouldn't ask Will to do that!

'*Would* you mind doing something wonderful for us so that we can run through this scene properly? If you could act as Kathy's hero just for this evening it would be so kind! You see, we could run through all the moves!'

Will flicked a look at Kathy's frozen face and grinned. He gave a little bow towards Molly. 'I'd be delighted,' he murmured. 'I'll do whatever you tell me!'

Molly clapped her hands in satisfaction. 'Great! Everybody, quiet! Will here is very sweetly going to take our hero's part tonight so that Kathy can get all her moves right. Take your places, please, and let's go from the top!'

Kathy flashed a glance at Will's enigmatic face. You're enjoying this, she thought furiously. How... how *could* she act opposite this man who had filled her every waking thought for the last few days? She felt confused and embarrassed. It was bad enough keeping her conflicting emotions at bay when she was working. How difficult would it be in this totally different social environment? She swallowed and started to speak the first lines...

The scene was nearly at an end. Never had Kathy wished so much for an evening to finish quickly. There seemed to be a great many moves which involved the hero putting his arm around her—when Will's broad chest was pressed against hers, or his cheek with its rough, end-of-day stubble was next to her soft skin. In his casual clothes he seemed even taller and broader than at work—or was it because she had never been this near to him? She was aware as never before of his physical presence.

Will seemed to throw himself into the part. When Molly suggested he pull Kathy towards him and cradle her in his arms he did it with enthusiasm, although Kathy did her best to hold back. Several times Molly called out, 'Kathy, you're standing too far away from the hero—move closer, dear.'

Kathy would do so reluctantly. This 'acting' was becoming too real for her! If she hadn't felt so physically attracted to him, didn't work so closely with him, it wouldn't have mattered. As it was, she felt Will was only too aware of the reason for her unwillingness—and he was relishing every moment!

'And now,' called out Molly, 'we're coming to the climax of the scene, which, of course, is *most* important. When the hero kisses the heroine it must be deliberate and sudden, and although the heroine is startled she capitulates. Perhaps she has begun to realise that she might love him just a little.'

Kathy felt a flutter of horror. 'Oh, Molly, can't we just leave that part out?' she pleaded rather desperately. 'I mean, surely it's better to leave this bit until Peter can be here and do it properly with me—I'll only have to do it all over again with him. Will's so much taller than Peter that I might get my moves wrong or something…'

Her voice tailed off rather tamely and her eye caught Will's glance for a second. An amused smile played round his lips and she knew he was aware that she wanted to put distance between them.

Molly shrugged. 'If you really want to wait, that's OK. I must say one can't go through one's moves too much really…'

'I couldn't agree with you more.'

Kathy jumped at the sound of Will's deep voice, and then, before she knew what was happening, his arms were around her and his mouth was pressing firmly on her lips, his breath on her cheek. Her lips tingled with the feel of his firm mouth on hers, electric shocks of attraction crackling crazily through her body. Most insidious was the response of her own body, her lips starting to part softly under his insistent mouth. Instinctively, and treacherously, her arms wound round his neck and she felt a thrill of desire as his hard body pressed against hers.

This was insane! Her heart hammered so hard she could hardly breathe and she felt the conflicting emotions of embarrassment, shock and, undeniably and forcefully, the animal attraction of Will Curtis.

For a few seconds she was completely enfolded by him, mentally and physically, then with a supreme effort she pushed him away from her as hard as she could. Breathlessly they stood slightly apart, Will looking down at her with an unfathomable look in his eyes, Kathy looking back at him completely dazed.

His hands were still on her shoulders and she felt powerless to move. He brought his hand up to brush her cheek and a sudden amused grin lit his face.

'I didn't know acting could be such fun,' he murmured, his eyes laughing at her mischievously.

He knows I responded to him! Kathy's face burned in an agony of embarrassment. She took a deep breath and tried to ignore the thudding of her heart and the trembling in her knees. She was damn well going to show Will Curtis that she hadn't been affected in any way by his 'stage' kiss!

She looked pointedly at her watch. 'It's getting late,' she observed lightly, trying to keep her voice steady. 'I'll have to fly. I want to go and see Peter—make sure he's up to coming to the next rehearsal!'

That should tell Will, she reflected with satisfaction, make him realise who I'd *rather* be acting with!

Molly bustled up, waving her scripts at them excitedly. 'That was excellent!' she boomed. 'You know, Will, I have to say that if we hadn't cast the hero already you would have been a very good choice!'

Kathy glowered at her, then walked quickly over to

the cloakroom to get her coat, where she sank shakily onto a bench. Blast Will Curtis! She could hardly admit it to herself, but that kiss had shaken her to the core. Oh, it was true that from the first moment she'd ever clapped eyes on him she'd felt a frisson of attraction dart through her, but now she knew what it actually felt like to have his lips on hers, she realised that it had become full-blooded desire—and with the one man in the world she had never wanted to work with!

What was even worse, Kathy reflected, Will seemed to regard their relationship as something of a joke. Sometimes when he looked at her she had thought there was more than banter behind his words. She was wrong, she thought crossly. The rehearsal had shown her that he took a very light-hearted view of their association. If only she hadn't responded so eagerly to that cheeky kiss of his!

Will was waiting for her on the steps outside.

'Can I give my leading lady a lift?' he enquired softly, a grin flashing across his face.

Kathy flashed angry eyes at him. He must be thinking what a huge laugh this was—her inadequate acting and the fact she was obviously embarrassed by the whole situation!

'It's quite all right. As I said, I'm going to see how Peter is—see if I can give him a lift to the next rehearsal.' She'd said that rather pointedly, and added firmly, 'Anyway, I need some fresh air.'

He looked up at the dark, cloudy sky. It was raining quite steadily. 'You're going to get pretty wet—are you sure?'

'Absolutely!' Kathy tried to inject enthusiasm into her voice. 'I'll see you tomorrow, then. Bye!'

She marched briskly off down the rain-soaked road,

her heart hammering. She heard Will's deep chuckle behind her. 'Goodnight, Sarah Bernhardt...sleep tight!'

Will watched Kathy's tall figure as she disappeared into the darkness, the drops of heavy drizzle sparkling in the light of the streetlamps and throwing a glow of gold onto her honey-coloured hair. His expression changed and a strangely bitter twist came to his lips, his hands clenching tensely by his sides.

'If only I could tell her,' he muttered. 'If only I hadn't promised Dad and Randolph not to say why the land is being sold... She'd understand, surely she would!'

Then he shook his head and sighed. 'I'm a fool,' he whispered angrily to himself. 'I can't tell her—and yet she's so damn beautiful. I was an idiot to lose control and kiss her like that. She doesn't trust me as it is.'

He kicked a stone moodily into the road. He'd made too many sacrifices over the last few months—he was damned if he was going to sacrifice a future with a girl he hadn't been able to stop thinking about since he'd first seen her. Kathy Macdowell had knocked him sideways and somehow, in some way, despite the circumstances, he was going to win her.

He hunched his jacket up round his ears, pushed his hands dejectedly into his pockets and walked slowly back to his car. He turned the key in the door and looked down the street again.

'One day,' he promised himself. 'One day, when she knows me better and things have sorted themselves out, one day...!'

CHAPTER FIVE

KATHY was late—very late. She should never have taken the phone call, but when Ruth had told her it was her cousin, John Macdowell, on the line, she hadn't had the heart to say she was just going out.

He'd sounded rather desperate, his gruff voice shouting loudly down the phone.

'I've finally decided, Kathy. I can't take any more of this damn hassle from Randolph Curtis. I'm selling up!'

Kathy was stunned. The farm had been in their family for several generations, and it had been her cousin's life—or so she'd thought.

'You *can't* make hasty decisions like that,' she'd protested. 'You love the farm—surely there must be a way to go on without the land you want from Randolph Curtis?'

'The blasted man wants me out. He wants to buy the place and sell it on, I'm sure,' growled John.

'Then why give him that satisfaction?' demanded Kathy irritably. Really, she began to feel her cousin was being wimpish, although she was equally cross with Randolph for causing such bother in the first place.

She tried to calm the situation. 'Look, John,' she said pacifyingly, 'why don't I come over later and we can discuss the options a little more fully? It's difficult when you've no one to talk to at the farm...'

'Yes, that would help,' conceded John gruffly. 'I'd like your opinion, Kathy.'

And now, thought Kathy crossly as she crashed the gears and turned into the car park of Bentham Infirmary, she'd used up a large chunk of her precious lunch-hour talking to her cousin when she should have been visiting her old partner, Harry Lord.

Talk about hassle, she fumed as she just managed to beat another car into the last remaining space. The Curtis family seemed adept at causing ructions in her family one way or another. Randolph was a powerful man, quite ready to have his own way and ride rough-shod over people. Didn't she know that only too well from that sad little entry in her mother's diary?

Now the next generation of Curtises was at it—only this time causing disruption in *her* life! A picture of herself and Will at the rehearsal flew into her mind, and she shuddered. How embarrassing an experience *that* had been! He had seemed to delight in teasing her. What a pity she had responded so seriously to his stage kiss!

Now she wanted to reassure Harry, recovering from his triple bypass operation, that she was coping magnificently without him, and that there was no need for him to worry about the practice at all or to come back before he was ready!

It wasn't exactly the impression she was likely to give Harry, she thought wryly. A glance in the car mirror revealed her hot, flushed cheeks and ragged hair. Far from looking calm, she gave the impression of having run all the way from the surgery to the hospital! A busy morning, culminating in that phone call, had wrought havoc with her looks.

She dragged a comb quickly through her hair and

decided firmly that soon, very soon, she would have the lot cut off. She was sick of the thick pleat she wore at work coming loose and falling down round her shoulders—perhaps it was time for a change of image! She strode off quickly down the corridor.

Reaching the coronary care unit, Kathy peered with slight trepidation around the corner of the amenity room where Harry was ensconced. He'd had a slight infection and that had delayed his recovery, but he looked up and waved at her enthusiastically to come in, and she saw with relief that he looked quite robust.

He grinned at her. 'Don't look so apprehensive— I'm not quite on my last legs,' he joked.

Kathy plonked herself down on the chair by his bed. 'Thank God you're OK. I believe you had an infection and I was a bit worried, but you look really great. You've got more colour in your cheeks than when I last saw you!'

'I always blush when a beautiful girl visits me,' Harry asserted solemnly.

Kathy made a face at him. 'You must be feeling better! Seriously, though, is it very painful?'

Harry shook his head. 'No, it's not too bad.' He pulled open his pyjama top and revealed a long scar down the centre of his chest. 'Look at that neat zipper incision! It's just a little unnerving when I feel the wire click that's holding the breastbone. Where they took the veins out of my leg it's a bit painful, but I'm pretty sure I'll be back part time in six weeks. And I'll tell you something—my circulation's improved a lot. My hands are much warmer!'

Kathy frowned at him severely. It had taken some time for Harry to realise, or admit to the fact, that he'd needed medical attention. Now he needed time to get back on his feet.

'Harry, don't be absurd. You promised Val that you'd take at least three months off after the hard time we had, getting you to see anybody, and you, of all people, should have known better than to keep your health worries to yourself.'

'She's a dragon, my wife—and so are you,' said Harry ruefully. He looked quizzically at Kathy. 'Talking of dragons, what about William Curtis? Did my choice turn out to be the nightmare you thought? Is he as arrogant as you say his uncle is?'

Kathy flushed slightly. 'No...no, he's a most efficient man. Good at his job, the patients like him...'

And I like him too much, she admitted to herself, despite what his uncle had done to her family, despite some of the things about Will's private life that puzzled her and despite that light and jokey attitude to her, half flirting, half mocking. Harry Lord could never even come close to guessing what her true feelings were for Will Curtis!

'You see,' Harry continued ruefully, 'I've been feeling guilty about going over your head and employing him. I was getting a bit panicky about leaving you alone in the practice, and perhaps I plunged in a bit recklessly there. It could make for awful problems if you can't get on with the man.'

'No, no,' soothed Kathy lightly. 'We've, er, got along fine, in the circumstances. I just try to keep off the subject of holiday leisure centres!'

'So you've no worries about your relationship with him, then?' persisted Harry.

Kathy bit her lip. It was their relationship that seemed to take up most of her thoughts at the moment—the fact that she seemed to be falling in love with the man, and he, well, she couldn't tell what he thought of her!

'He's a good doctor, very supportive...' she said briefly.

Harry laughed. 'So I'm not being missed at the moment. Sounds as if Will's doing his fair share of work. I'm relieved! I thought he was an excellent candidate and just right for our practice, but it seemed almost too good to be true that he'd decided to settle here because of his father's problems.'

Kathy looked at him reflectively. 'Did he expand on those problems?' she asked.

'Not really. I gather his father's health isn't very good, but Will just said he had to help his father unravel a few difficulties. I wondered if he wasn't being impetuous in giving up his job in Africa for what sounded like a short-term thing. Perhaps he's a bit impulsive on occasion.'

Yes, certainly impulsive on occasion! Kathy suppressed a nervous giggle and nodded. 'He's full of energy. In fact, I think you'll have something of a shock when you see the centre!'

Harry looked slightly alarmed. 'What's he been doing to it? Nothing too radical, I hope!'

'He got sick of me banging my car on that awkward tree so he's reorganised the parking—the lines have been repainted. And he's something of a landscape gardener. The front patch is glowing with bedding-out plants!'

She decided not to tell him about the complete redecoration of the surgery after the flood, or the replacement of a lot of the timber in the loft—one thing at a time! Harry was a naturally conservative sort of man and his blood pressure might rise alarmingly if he knew the full extent of the changes that had been made!

How different from Will Curtis! In a short time the medical centre had been transformed, and Kathy couldn't help but feel proud of the place every time she came to work.

Harry sniffed rather deprecatingly. 'Hope he hasn't tarted up the place too much. It's a medical practice, not a garden centre!'

'Don't worry.' She smiled. 'I think you'll be impressed.'

'As long as you're managing to rub along with him all right,' remarked Harry. 'He had such an outstanding CV. I thought that you'd probably get on professionally. And he's not a bad-looking young man, is he?' he added with a wicked grin.

'I hadn't noticed,' replied Kathy a little too quickly, flicking back a strand of hair rather too casually.

The trouble was, thought Kathy ruefully a few minutes later as she walked briskly down the hospital corridor, that Will Curtis seemed to pop up everywhere—from the gym to the play rehearsal! It was getting harder and harder to avoid the man—and to suppress feelings that she felt guilty about having! A Curtis wasn't to be trusted, as her mother had discovered, and that was a powerful reason to avoid a relationship.

She reflected that two men couldn't have been more different than Harry Lord and Will Curtis. Even before he'd become ill, Harry had liked to live life at a snail's pace. Will seemed like a ball of fire compared to him. When Harry did come back to work it would be rather interesting to see how he would tolerate Will's multitude of ideas, not least building onto the existing centre and having a physiotherapist and chiropodist part time!

Kathy glanced at her watch and decided there was time to have a bite of lunch, before returning to the surgery. It might be quicker to go to the hospital canteen and she could reflect on what her cousin had had to say about leaving the farm. She remembered what Randolph Curtis had once said about John—that he was hitting the bottle and wasn't capable of running the place. Although she'd dismissed the idea angrily at the time, reluctantly she'd begun to wonder if there wasn't a grain of truth in it. Her cousin *had* sounded a little incoherent and rambling on the phone. She sighed. She'd find out later that afternoon.

Two men came out of a side corridor and turned towards her, deep in conversation. Her heart fluttered. There was no mistaking the tall figure of one of them— Will Curtis. Darn the man! He was probably visiting a patient, so it wasn't surprising to see him there. All the same, she was suddenly aware she didn't look her best... The work suit she had on had seen rather a lot of service, and seemed mysteriously to have shrunk slightly—or perhaps she was developing new muscles in her regime at the gym! Surreptitiously she smoothed down the jacket over her curves and held back her shoulders.

He looked up as they passed. Naturally, he saw her and his brows shot up in surprise, his intense blue eyes locking with hers for a second. He stopped in front of her, blocking her path.

'Can't get away from each other, can we?' he murmured with a humorous twitch of his lips. He turned to the man beside him. 'Kathy's a leading lady in the local dramatic society. I'm only doing the scenery, but

I was lucky enough to stand in for the hero the other night!' His eyes danced. 'It was good fun, wasn't it? I must say I never thought I'd enjoy acting so much!'

Kathy blushed a deep pink, but Will seemed unaware of her embarrassment.

'This is Kevin Stuart, who repaired Randolph's hernia. You probably know each other, anyway. I've just been in to see the old boy. He's not in the best of moods—post-operative bad temper, I think!'

Kathy and Kevin Stuart nodded and smiled at each other. Kathy frequently referred patients to him when they had to have general surgery.

'So, is Randolph doing all right?' she enquired politely.

'Being a bloody difficult patient,' said Will with a laugh.

'I can certainly imagine that!' declared Kathy with feeling. 'He made enough fuss about letting us get him to hospital, although he was pretty ill.'

'He wasn't too good when he was brought in,' observed Kevin. 'It was lucky you got to him when you did, but he should be fine in a few weeks if he takes it easy—although, knowing Randolph Curtis, I doubt he knows how to do that!'

He shot a look at his watch. 'Hope you'll excuse me. I must be going now. Sorry to shoot off so quickly.' He grinned at them. 'I've got a hot date with the new woman in my life!'

He gave Will a friendly punch on the shoulder. 'About time you started following my example, Will. You're going to be an old man soon and get left behind! There are too many of you bachelors floating around, enjoying yourselves!'

With a wave he marched quickly off down the corridor.

Kathy looked questioningly up at Will. 'Who's his new woman?' she asked.

He chuckled. 'Kevin's wife's just had a baby girl—their first daughter—and she's in the maternity wing at the moment.' He looked with amusement at Kevin's vanishing figure. 'I've never known a man so excited, although he's got two little boys already. He's a real family man is Kevin, and loves every minute of it!'

'You sound rather envious,' said Kathy. 'Or were you just being sarcastic?'

Will smiled wistfully. 'No, I meant it. I think perhaps I am a little envious. There may be compensations for being tied down, as it were—stability, looking after someone other than oneself…'

His eyes held hers for a second, and he frowned slightly. 'Nobody's managed to capture you, then, Kathy? You haven't been tempted to settle down?'

There was a seriousness in his voice, but when she looked at him again his eyes were twinkling and his tone had become jocular. 'You're probably so busy fighting men off, you've not thought about it!'

Not thought about it! It had been so long since a man who'd attracted her had looked at her with any kind of interest! Oh, there'd been casual dates with pleasant men in the past, but life had been hectic, bringing up Lindy over the past two years after their mother's death. It had also been rather serious, with not much time for fun or thinking of her own enjoyment. That was why, a small voice said in her brain, meeting someone like Will Curtis had come as such a thunderbolt—and perhaps why she felt so unable to handle it.

She gave a casual laugh and said lightly, 'Good Lord, I've had no time for that sort of thing. Looking after a young sister and helping to run a practice is quite time-consuming, you know!'

He nodded, as if dismissing the subject, and turned to her with a smile. 'Fancy some lunch in the canteen here? There's a patient I'd like to talk to you about—now might be a good opportunity, instead of going back to the surgery.'

Kathy hesitated. Lunchtime was an ideal time to discuss aspects of the practice, but since the embarrassment of the rehearsal she was loath to spend much time alone with Will. Then she shrugged. She was being silly—the man was asking her to have lunch in a professional capacity, for heaven's sake, not trying to manoeuvre her into another heart-stopping kiss!

She nodded and followed him into the canteen.

The sandwiches were the usual Bentham Infirmary fare—thick bread with tasteless fillings, slightly curling at the edges.

Will made a face after the first mouthful. 'Next time we eat out I'll try and do better for you than this.' He took a sip of coffee. 'God—instant sludge! How do they do it?'

Kathy giggled and pointed to a poster on the wall depicting a delighted-looking woman brandishing a large cake. A balloon came out of her mouth with the words, 'Bentham Infirmary Canteen—voted the best food in the county'!

Will raised his eyebrows. 'Don't know who did the voting—not the diners, that's for sure!'

His expression changed from humorous to grave and he pushed his plate away, leaning forward on his elbows. 'Do you know a patient called Gary Layton—about sixteen?'

Kathy nodded. 'I know who you mean. I think he's Harry's patient so I've never dealt with him. He's Annie Forster's grandson—the woman who was mugged and you cut the ring off her finger. Pat Layton's his mother—she's a patient of mine. She changed to me because she preferred a woman doctor. Is there a problem with Gary?'

'Could be a big one,' said Will grimly, putting a large spoonful of sugar into his coffee and stirring it absently. 'He's on heroin—says he's desperate to come off and wants me to put him on a reducing regime of methadone for withdrawal.'

Kathy gave a quick, shocked intake of breath. 'I can't believe it!' she whispered. 'He's come from such a stable family background. His father's a successful businessman and Pat Layton's a pillar of the community—it just shows no one's immune. Do you think he's told his parents?'

'No, I'm sure he hasn't. I told him that he would have to be registered with the Home Office as a drug user, but he kept wanting to be reassured that everything would be confidential.'

Kathy thought of Pat's appointment with her and a picture of her agitated manner flashed into her mind.

'I wonder…' she murmured. 'She came into the surgery last week, feeling tired and generally under the weather. I sent her for blood tests and she's due to see me again this week. I have to admit I felt she had some underlying worries—although she assured me she hadn't. Perhaps she does suspect all isn't well. What have you decided to do about the boy?'

Will shook his head. 'I don't know. I think he's try-ing to bamboozle me a bit. Swears, of course, that he'll try very hard. Says he's never been on rehab before. I'm not convinced. I'm wondering where he gets his money from and if he's just going to sell on the meth-adone to feed his heroin habit.'

'That's always a danger,' agreed Kathy.

Will paused and frowned. 'I think he's hiding some-thing from me. He tried to be very conciliatory and convincing, but underneath there was a lot of agitation. I felt he was frightened, very frightened.'

'Perhaps the effects of his last fix were wearing off?'

'Could be,' Will conceded. 'I asked him what had made him decide to go for rehab. He looked a bit jumpy and said he knew it was wrong to take drugs and he wanted to get his life straight—but I felt there was more to it than that. Anyway, I explained that sticking to a programme wasn't easy and that he would have to sign a ''contract'' with me to fulfil his part of the bargain—that was, to come back each week and have random urine tests to ensure that he's staying off the heroin.'

'Did he accept that?'

Will shrugged. 'Oh, yes, very quickly, but when I told him to come back tomorrow for my decision he became sullen, even abusive, and was adamant he needed to go on it that very minute! I wanted to know if you knew anything more about the lad.'

'Afraid not—only his background. What school's he at?'

'He was at the local comprehensive, but he says he's left and is looking for a job.'

'That's Lindy's school,' said Kathy, 'and she's about his age. Of course, I can't say anything to her about him, but I could ask if she's aware of any drugs being pushed at school.' She looked reflectively at Will. 'It's ironic. The Laytons seem such a model family—no money worries, parents involved in their children's welfare. I wonder what went wrong?'

Will sighed and shook his head. 'I suppose there are quite a few reasons for starting drugs—peer pressure, some momentary hiccup that makes them vulnerable. Whatever, I hate to think of that young man starting down the slippery slope so early.'

His mouth thinned and hardened. 'What wouldn't I do to the creeps who hook these kids on these drugs and then have them at their mercy…?'

He was silent for a second, then his face lit with a companionable smile. 'Thanks for giving me the time—I appreciate it.'

He looked at the sandwich she'd left uneaten on her plate and the cup of cold coffee barely tasted.

'I see you've enjoyed the cuisine here as much as I have. Look, the food in this area can't all be like this. Can you recommend anywhere that does something eatable?'

Kathy laughed. 'Plenty of places! Personally, I like a little pub, The Jolly Miller. It's just near your barge, farther down the canal.'

'Good!' said Will briskly. 'Then we'll go at the weekend if you're free!'

'Oh, no, I didn't mean I wanted you to take me there,' she said quickly, her face flushing slightly. 'It's just a good place, that's all… Anyway, my evenings are filled up this weekend.'

She certainly wasn't going to get involved socially. Having to suppress her feelings for him at work was going to be difficult enough, and after all, she reminded herself sternly, he *was* a Curtis!

He looked at her unblinkingly and with an unmistakably stubborn expression that told her he wasn't so easily put off and reminded her just what family he came from!

'Very well. When's your first free evening? I hate eating on my own—and I don't know many people round here, you know. Go on,' he said in a persuasive tone, those amazing eyes dancing, 'I need someone local to tell me about the area. Besides, I want to know more about my practice partner—I don't like working in a vacuum.'

'I'd have thought your uncle could have told you all about Bentham,' she said brusquely.

'But I don't want to have dinner with Randolph,' he objected reasonably. 'I want to have dinner with someone who...' His eyes darkened as he looked at her under his brows. 'Someone who has something fresh to say and is more decorative to look at than my uncle.'

And that's precisely it, thought Kathy with a flash of irritation. He wants a reasonably attractive girl on hand and he doesn't know anyone but me—so I'll fill the bill, I suppose. The only thing is, I have a horrible feeling that too much of this particular Curtis will mean I end up with a broken heart—like my mother before me.

'I...I'll have to see,' she said lamely. 'I'll let you know when I know what Lindy's doing.'

He gave one of his devastating grins—a flash of white teeth and a humorous tilt of his brows.

'I'll have to be satisfied with that, then—for the moment.' He stood up and looked down at her, his blue eyes suddenly intent. 'Don't jump to too many conclusions about me,' he said lightly. 'Sometimes the Curtises have been known to be almost human... I'll see you later.'

Kathy felt her cheeks redden. His remarks had been too close to the mark for comfort, she reflected ruefully. Was she judging Will Curtis too much on her knowledge of his uncle? She sighed as she watched him making his way briskly away through the canteen. It was noticeable the way the women turned their heads as he passed, his tall physique and startling looks attracting their attention. He seemed oblivious to the fact that the blood pressure of most of the females in the room had gone up several points—except hers, Kathy told herself firmly!

Kathy spent the afternoon making some house calls, and after the last one she rang in to the surgery and told Ruth she was going to see her cousin, John Macdowell. She was worried about him. He had sounded a little incoherent on the phone when he'd been telling her he'd decided to give up the farm. She wanted to see for herself how things were.

John and she had been close. Their fathers were brothers, and when Kathy's father had died seventeen years ago, just before Lindy was born, John had done everything he could to help her mother. He was a lot older than Kathy, and things hadn't been easy for him. He had never married, and presented a rather lonely picture to the outside world.

Apprehensively, Kathy drove up the rutted drive to the old farmhouse.

There was no doubt that things had been allowed to drift, she thought, gazing at the barn at the side of the yard, its roof in sad need of repair and the door hanging off its hinges. It was basically an arable farm, and John was tinkering with the engine of a rusting tractor parked near the house.

He came towards her, wiping his hands on an oily rag. He looked much older, thought Kathy sadly. A few years ago he had been a well set-up, robust man. Now he looked smaller, slightly unkempt, a shadow of stubble on his unshaven chin.

'I was sorry to get your phone call, John. You sounded very upset.'

'Aye,' growled her cousin, nodding his head slowly. 'That damn Curtis—says there's no question of me having any more land adjacent to my bottom fields. Offered me some acres round the other side of the hill. Why should I take that?'

'So he did offer you some land, then?' said Kathy, surprised. Randolph Curtis must have softened somewhat in his attitude. 'I thought you weren't going to get anything at all. Won't that be any good?'

John Macdowell's face darkened. 'It's bloody inconvenient,' he grunted.

'But it is *something*,' argued Kathy persuasively. 'Surely you wouldn't give up the farm just because the new fields are a little way down the road?'

He looked at her belligerently. 'Whose side are you on?' he grated. 'I hear Curtis has his nephew working at the practice, so I suppose you're supporting him now?'

'Don't be ridiculous, John,' snapped Kathy crossly. She caught the sharp smell of alcohol on his breath— and she saw the tremble of his hands as he took a cigarette out of a pack and tried to light it. 'Have you had any lunch?' she asked more gently. 'Let's go in and have a cup of tea or something, and you can tell me your plans.'

John led the way silently into the house, and Kathy caught her breath when she saw the mess in the kitchen. She looked at the piles of dirty crockery by the sink and a heap of clothes in a corner. He had been a neat, fastidious man. What had gone wrong? In a relatively short time the place seemed to have gone downhill.

She filled a kettle with water and gestured to him to sit down. 'How are you feeling, John? You look as if you've lost weight. Is there anything the matter?'

He sat hunched in the chair for a moment, then put a hand up to his brow and nodded slowly, looking at Kathy rather miserably. 'Sorry I was a bit off with you, Kathy. I've not been quite straight with you. I suppose I'm ashamed...'

He gestured vaguely around the kitchen. 'I've let the place go, I know.' He hesitated for a moment, then said sadly, 'The truth is, my heart isn't in the farm any longer. Curtis *did* offer me land—quite good land—but it wasn't next door to my fields. That seemed to give me an excuse to get rid of the farm.'

'But *why*?'

John gave a tired smile. 'If I'd had a family perhaps, someone to pass the place on to, maybe I'd see some point in carrying on. As it is, I feel life is passing me by. I'd like to travel, see the world a bit, but leaving the farm to its own devices is difficult.'

Kathy nodded. 'I can understand that. You want to retire—and why not?'

Her cousin shrugged sadly. 'I feel perhaps I'm letting down my parents somehow, and the generations before that have worked down the years to keep the farm going. When Curtis refused me the land I wanted, in a funny sort of way it was a relief. I could retire and make it seem it was his fault I was doing so!'

'But now he's offered you some other land it's made you feel you'll have to keep going?'

'I suppose so,' he conceded. 'I would have been sorry to sell the farm, but if I had I'd have used the money to go round the world.'

'Well, why don't you sell it?' said Kathy briskly, pouring water from the kettle into the teapot. 'To hell with other generations. It would be better than sitting here, longing to do something else. And,' she added sternly, picking up a half-empty bottle of whisky on the draining-board, 'drinking yourself to death!'

He looked slightly shame-faced. 'I know, I know,' he admitted. 'I shouldn't be doing it, but it helps me get through the day.'

He was silent for a moment, taking the cup of tea she proffered him and sipping it slowly. 'So you don't think I'd be a fool to put it on the market?'

'Of course not.' Kathy smiled. 'Your life is your own—do something positive with it. You've worked long enough on your own.' She gazed out of the window and frowned slightly. 'I must say I'm amazed that Randolph Curtis offered you any land at all. What's come over him?'

'Perhaps he felt he was being a bit harsh. I thought perhaps he'd always resented the fact that this farm was owned by our family, although it was in the middle of his land, but I don't think that's the case. He just needs the land directly around mine for this leisure park business.'

'*That's* what baffles me,' said Kathy, shaking her head. 'I know he loves his land—why let it go? There

are various reasons why I don't like the man, but I
never thought he would give up his land.'

She stood up and went over to John and hugged him.
'Now, don't feel guilty because you want to have some
fun, but don't do anything in a hurry. Why not lease
your farm for a while, do your own thing? Then if you
feel you want to come back after a break of say, three
years, you can do so.'

John Macdowell grinned and suddenly looked about
ten years younger. 'I might have known you'd come
up with a good idea,' he said happily. 'I might just do
that!'

CHAPTER SIX

SUNLIGHT filtered through the half-open curtains in Kathy's bedroom, and she stretched lazily, watching the motes of dust dance in the beam of light. Wonderful! A Saturday morning with nothing to do. Will was doing the emergency surgery and one of the other practices in Bentham was on call over the weekend.

She drew back the curtain and sighed with satisfaction—a lovely day to herself. She would do some gardening and take Rafter for a walk over the fields. She wondered how long it would be before Randolph Curtis completed the sale of the land and the fields reaching down to the outskirts of Bentham were encased behind fences. The view she had now of hedges beautifully decked with may blossom and the glint of the canal might disappear for ever... Then she shrugged her shoulders irritably. Today she was going to relax and enjoy the countryside whilst she could, and not even think about the Curtis family—especially one William Curtis!

Lindy had gone up to the stables and was probably exercising Randolph's horse. Kathy frowned slightly. She could have wished that Lindy had chosen to help at stables other than his, but her sister did love going there, and it was true that Randolph seemed to be kind and generous to her, especially where payment for her help was concerned.

Slipping into some shorts and a crisp cotton shirt, Kathy made herself a cup of coffee and sauntered out into the little garden at the back of the house. She would sit down and decide just what needed doing first—perhaps some weeding, or filling the tubs with bright busy Lizzies. She certainly wouldn't think of anything to do with patients! Fleetingly her conversation with Will the other day regarding Gary Layton and his drug-taking activities came into her mind, then she firmly dismissed the thought and sank into the old hammock slung between two gnarled apple trees.

Dreamily she watched the branches swing up and down before her. It was very comfortable and rather warm, the sunlight dappled through the leaves, the sound of birdsong as a background. The practice and its worries seemed very far away...

Will lifted the heavy basket easily into the boot of his car. It was surprising what a bottle of wine, some chicken, smoked salmon and fruit could weigh!

He turned to Betty Cooper, Randolph's housekeeper, and gave her a light hug. 'You're a star, Betty. It looks fantastic and there's enough here to feed an army! I'm very grateful. Left to me, there might have been a stale pie and pickles!'

Betty laughed. 'You've got a lovely day for a picnic—mind you eat it all up! Three of you should be able to manage it with no difficulty! Lindy said she'd meet you by the barge, didn't she? Just have a lovely day—it's about time those girls enjoyed themselves!'

Will eased the car into gear and accelerated down the drive with a wave to Betty. If only I could be sure there will be three of us, he thought glumly, but nothing was too predictable where Kathy Macdowell was concerned! She wasn't aware yet that she was coming on his picnic and he wasn't convinced that his powers of persuasion would be sufficient for her to come! Perhaps the fact that Lindy had enthusiastically agreed to join them would help.

He'd had the idea of a picnic when he'd finished surgery and gone up to his uncle's house to make sure all was well. It wasn't often that good weather coincided with a weekend. Kathy had told him she couldn't come out in the evening so he'd spike her guns by taking her and her sister out in the daytime!

His eyes darkened as he pictured Kathy's tall, athletic body and her mane of honey-coloured hair. He'd had many girlfriends since medical school, but Kathy was something special, unique. Of course, he thought wryly, he'd known it since their very first meeting— almost as soon as he'd seen her walking her dog as he'd come over the brow of the hill. She just had to be the girl he'd been looking for and had never found—and the knowledge had hit him like a sledge-hammer! The fact that he'd found himself in the same practice as her had seemed a bonus at the time.

Kathy's image had been dancing in his mind far too much—and he knew time was against him. Unless he won her heart before the land was sold, he had no chance with her at all. She'd never look at anyone connected with the Curtis family after that—and how could he work with her then, let alone hope that she'd care for him?

He scowled fiercely at the scenery as he sped along. He had some sympathy with Kathy's point of view regarding the sale of the land, but it was the only thing his uncle could do in the peculiar circumstances in which they found themselves. He gripped the steering-wheel tightly. He hadn't planned to get involved with anyone—not until the problem with his father had been resolved. Now, like a fool, he'd fallen for the girl most likely to turn him down!

Kathy stirred lightly. It had been impossible not to drift off to sleep, with the warm sun filtering through the branches of the trees and the gently swaying motion of the hammock. She had been having the most delightful dream. She had seemed to be at another rehearsal, and the producer had insisted that she and Will Curtis practise the kiss scene together. It was very enjoyable and sweet, and Will had demanded that they keep repeating the performance…

A fly seemed to be pestering her, tickling her nose and teasing her awake. She brushed it aside irritably—she wasn't ready to wake from the dream yet! Still it persisted, and Kathy's eyes flew open in exasperation and looked straight into a familiar pair of blue eyes fringed with black lashes. Will Curtis was about two feet from her!

She gave a little scream. 'What on earth are you doing?' she yelped. The hammock swung over and dumped her on the grass so that she sprawled in an undignified way at his feet, her hair spread out, tumbled and disarrayed.

He laughed and hauled her up with a strong hand.

'You must have been having nice thoughts—you had a smile on your face! Did I startle you?' His eyes danced at her before sweeping over her tall figure, lingering for an appreciative second on her long legs in the decidedly short shorts.

'Of course you did!' Kathy felt flustered and flushed hotly, not least because she'd just been dreaming of the damn man and he'd come closer to the truth than he could have imagined! 'What is it? Has something gone wrong at the surgery?'

'No, nothing like that,' he said soothingly, 'but we're due to meet Lindy at the barge in ten minutes. I've persuaded her to have a picnic with us...'

'Lindy? What's Lindy got to do with it?' Still dazed from sleep, Kathy's emerald eyes widened in puzzlement.

He grinned. 'I thought you'd be more likely to come with me if Lindy came—and, anyway, I wanted to thank her for dealing with my uncle when he was ill so I asked her when I was up at Randolph's house after work this morning.'

Kathy frowned. It sounded very devious to her—just another Curtis scheme! She looked at Will challengingly. 'I haven't agreed to go anywhere with you, have I?'

Will smiled at her and took her arm gently. 'Don't you remember? I said I wanted to take you out for a meal. Today's perfect—warm sun, a free afternoon and the dogs need a walk!'

'I don't understand... Have you got some food?'

He laughed. 'Have I got some food? It's ambrosial, food for the gods, and nectar in the shape of some very cool Frascati!'

She stared at him. 'But... I can't come. I've things to do—the garden, ironing...'

His hand slid down her arm and took her hand firmly in his. 'You don't want to disappoint your little sister, do you? Come on, Kathy—it could be raining tomorrow.'

His hand felt strong and unyielding. More than that, it made her whole body tingle. Suddenly, on this heavenly, balmy day, Kathy longed for him to pull her towards him and kiss her as he had the other evening, to feel the soft brush of his firm lips on hers...only that had just been 'fun' to him, hadn't it? It hadn't left him trembling and shaken with desire as she had been...

She tried to draw her hand away, but he held it fast and looked down at her sternly. 'Don't be a killjoy,' he said firmly. 'I've got food for about ten people in the car—you can't let it go to waste! Anyway, you practically promised me that you would have a proper meal with me after that horrible lunch in the hospital canteen!'

'I didn't promise! I said I *might*!' protested Kathy, half running behind him as he firmly towed her along.

He stopped suddenly as they reached the car, and she bumped hard into him so that he had to steady her with both hands. He looked down at her, mock severely. 'In my book, a promise is a promise, however you put it. Come on—Lindy will be waiting for us, and if I know teenage appetites she'll be ravenous!'

He opened the passenger door and Kathy slid in, murmuring, 'I look a sight. My hair's all over the place, and these shorts are—'

'Delightful!' he finished off for her with an appreciative grin.

He walked back and gave a low whistle, and a mournful Rafter, who had been watching them dolefully through the gate, gave a yelp of pleasure and raced through as Will opened it, landing on the back seat of the sports car with a scrabble of paws and fur.

Then, before Kathy could protest any further, Will started the car and shot off down the road.

It was lovely, sitting on the deck of the barge. Will had put out chairs and a wooden crate served as a table.

The sun warmed the planks beneath their feet, and the canal sparkled. Occasionally another barge would chug quietly by, and a small family of ducks swam busily up and down.

Magnus and Rafter lay at one end under the shade of the small cabin roof, panting vociferously and looking with liquid and longing brown eyes at the plates of cold salmon and chicken and the bowl of strawberries topped with thick clotted cream. Will had sternly forbidden them to come any nearer. Every now and then he gave a warning shout if they dared to edge closer.

'Mmm, this is heavenly,' murmured Kathy, having a deep sip of the cool, sparkling wine and looking lazily round at the view of rolling fields on one side of the canal and the abundant hedgerow with its filigree border of meadowsweet on the other side by the towpath. The sweet and elusive smell of may blossom and elderflower drifted over. She sighed with contentment and stretched her shapely legs on the side of the barge, her face shielded by the shade of the large straw hat she'd found in the little galley.

Kathy looked across at Lindy, who was sitting at the edge of the barge and dabbling her feet in the water. She was so glad that her sister was with them. Somehow the thought of being alone with Will Curtis was too disturbing. With Lindy there, she felt totally relaxed—why, she could almost put out of her mind that he was drop-dead gorgeous!

She smiled fondly at the teenager. Lindy might look a little…different, with her hair a rather startling shade of red at the moment and in tight little plaits around her head, but she was good fun and had a generous heart.

'I hope you haven't had too much wine, little sister,'

she remarked teasingly. 'You're in charge of a horse, remember!'

The horse was tethered at the side of the tow-path, cropping the lush grass there greedily.

Lindy's sunburnt face turned towards Kathy and she put her tongue out. 'Fusspot!' she said. 'Zephyr knows his own way home by now!' She stretched lazily and declared, 'I couldn't eat any more—I'm absolutely bursting! You're a great cook, Will!'

Will had been lying back in a battered old deckchair, his long legs spread in front of him, a baseball cap tipped over his eyes.

He chuckled. 'It was pretty easy for a man of my talents—I asked Betty to do us a snack. Good job I didn't ask for a big meal!'

'A pity I've got to get back,' said Lindy regretfully. 'Zephyr needs grooming, and I have to let the other horses out into the field. It's been great, Will—and I love your barge, with its dear little galley and bunks, and all the painting on the wood round the sides. I could live here for ever!'

Will grinned. 'It's probably more your size than mine. Sometimes I think I'm punch-drunk with the number of times I've hit my head on the roof, getting up in the mornings. I'm going to have to look for larger accommodation before I fracture my skull!'

'You ought to do a swop with our cousin,' said Lindy brightly. 'Your barge would suit him down to the ground. He could go round Britain's canals in it, couldn't he Kathy? And Will would love the farm.'

Kathy frowned crossly at Lindy. What a preposterous idea! But Will leaned forward with interest.

'Is this the cousin who's been driven out, you say, by Randolph because of a land dispute?'

Lindy nodded eagerly. 'That's right, but now he thinks it's given him a chance to do something he's always longed to do—go travelling.' She turned to Kathy enthusiastically. 'It's a brilliant idea of mine, isn't it? Will could lease John's house and that would solve loads of problems. The farmland could be let out.'

Kathy sighed. Somehow the Curtis family seemed to be getting even more enmeshed in her family's affairs.

'I suppose so,' she said cautiously.

Will flicked a quick look across at her—her reluctance must have been obvious to him. He gave a beguiling schoolboy grin.

'It could do no harm to ask,' he remarked lightly. 'Good thinking, Lindy. It could suit your cousin and me very well. There's just a chance that my father will be able to stay with me fairly soon—and somehow I don't think this barge would hold two large men! I don't think the chap it belongs to would have the slightest objection—he just wants the thing in use.'

Kathy looked sharply at him. Will rarely mentioned his father and didn't encourage questions about him, but there was a wistful expression on his face that belied his light-hearted comment.

'Would your father like living in a run-down old farmhouse?' she enquired tentatively.

'It would be heaven to him after what he's endured.' There was a finality about Will's comment. Kathy forbore to ask further questions.

Lindy stretched and yawned. 'Well, folks, I've got to go.' She leapt nimbly from the barge to the path. 'Thanks a ton—it's been really cool, this, Will. You'll have to come back to ours some time—Kathy and I could cook you up something good. See you!'

Kathy sat up in alarm as Lindy untethered Zephyr and sprang onto his broad back, suddenly aware that Will and she would be the only occupants of the barge. After all the wine she'd had, she didn't feel she could cope with his jokey flirting without seriously compromising herself!

'You don't have to go just yet, do you?' she said pleadingly. 'Surely the horse can wait an hour or so while we make a cup of tea…'

Her voice trailed away as with a backward cheery wave Lindy ambled off down the tow-path on Zephyr.

It was very quiet. Kathy lay back in her chair again and Will glanced at her profile—upturned nose under the big brim of the hat and tumbling hair brushing her shoulders.

'Good idea of mine, or what?' he murmured.

He saw a smile curve her cheek. 'Yes,' she admitted. 'I'm glad I came.'

She twisted in her chair and studied him for a moment. His strong, tanned legs were propped up on the makeshift table, a muscular forearm draped over the arm of the deckchair. Her breath caught in her throat. Oh, God, he looked so wonderful and she didn't know if she was comfortable, being so close to him on her own. Damn Lindy for leaving so thoughtlessly!

A heavy silence developed between them, and Kathy became more and more aware of his physical presence. She had to lighten the atmosphere, and say something inconsequential.

'Do you miss Africa?' she blurted out desperately.

He sat up and leaned forward, his elbows on his knees, his blue eyes dancing with amusement at her as if he knew why she'd spoken.

'I thought I would never settle here again. But, actually,' he added, 'I don't miss Africa as much as I thought I would. I love it here. Oh, I miss the people I met—there were some great characters out there, and I did feel we were getting our message across regarding child welfare. I shall definitely go back to see what progress they've made. It's a very beautiful country— but I guess I'm an Englishman at heart, and at the moment home is where the heart is!'

He stood up and took Kathy's glass, pouring some more wine into it, and looked down at her. 'And you, what about you, Kathy? Are you happy here? Is Bentham where you want to be?'

Kathy twirled the glass and watched the bubbles explode on the surface. She was beginning to feel slightly light-headed. 'Of course—I just wish it wasn't being pulled apart by your damned uncle. Bentham will never be the same to me when he's finished with it!'

For a second Will said nothing, but it suddenly seemed as if the temperature had dropped a few degrees. He turned towards her and frowned.

'For God's sake, Kathy, play a different tune. Can't you forget about Randolph and his land plans for a while?'

Kathy glanced at his exasperated expression and a wave of irritation flashed through her. Why shouldn't she mention what was uppermost in her mind?

'Of course I can't forget about this holiday centre,' she snapped, sitting up abruptly. 'Just look at the gorgeous scenery all around us—going to be desecrated for the sake of money. I can *never* forget about it!' she added passionately. 'It means everything to me. Generations of my family have farmed it—long before Sir Randolph bloody Curtis got his hands on it! Of course,

I don't expect you to understand—you don't care a fig what Randolph does!'

She stood up and pushed past him angrily, but he shot out a hand and held her fast.

'What do you know about anything?' he said harshly. 'As a matter of fact, my uncle is being totally unselfish in selling this land for reasons that I'm not prepared to divulge—and I *do* care, because I'm closely involved in it! Whatever happens, the money has to be raised!'

She stared at him. 'So, you're colluding with him, are you?' she said coldly. 'I might have known. Like uncle, like nephew—milking the land for money...'

They glared at each other. Her hair was disordered, tumbling about her shoulders, her cheeks pink with fury. His eyes raked her face and his mouth tightened.

'You know nothing about it,' he whispered.

He turned abruptly and watched a small group of people in shorts run past on the tow-path, their light-hearted banter filling the air. Kathy bit her lip and sighed inwardly. For some reason Will suddenly looked like a man with all the cares of the world on his shoulders, his head bowed and his hands clenched tightly.

What was it about this land deal that was making him so jumpy? Perhaps there really was some earth-shattering reason for the sale of the land. Whatever, when it came to that subject he had a complex and moody reaction that she couldn't understand. She was convinced there was something in his background that he was hiding from her.

Despite his response to her, however, Kathy felt slightly stricken with remorse. He'd gone to a lot of trouble to give Lindy and her a lovely afternoon, and she had spoilt it by mentioning his uncle's plans.

'I...I'm sorry,' she said contritely. 'Perhaps I went a bit over the top. I tend to do that where Randolph's concerned...'

'So I noticed.' Will's voice was terse, but he turned towards her and Kathy continued.

'You see, it's not just the land plans—there are other reasons for my wariness of him. Apart from the way he seemed to mess my cousin around, you don't know what he did to my mother...'

Will looked at her with a baffled expression. 'What the hell do you mean—did to your mother?'

'He made her very unhappy.'

Will raised his eyebrows. 'In what way? How could he do that?'

Kathy suddenly felt embarrassed. It had to be the wine talking—she definitely shouldn't be giving away family secrets to this man!

'It's nothing,' she muttered. 'I don't think it would interest you, anyway.'

'I don't understand,' he said more gently. 'I believe your mother died some time ago—long before this land sale came up. You're saying that Randolph hurt her in some other way? I wish you'd tell me...'

Kathy twisted a tendril of hair behind her ear and bit her lip. No one except her knew of that sad entry in her mother's diary, and the truth was that Kathy herself didn't really know exactly what it was that had caused her mother such pain—only that her sadness had been caused by Will Curtis's uncle. Even now, the words leapt off the page of the diary. 'No matter how he bullies me I will not give in...'

She reached forward and scratched Rafter's soft,

silky ears. 'As you say,' she said lightly, 'it was a long time ago, many years actually, and it should be water under the bridge now…'

His eyes narrowed. 'But you've never forgotten it, have you? There's more to your antipathy towards Randolph than the land issue,' he remarked shrewdly. 'And you don't want to tell me about it.'

'I can't really, even if I wanted to, because I only know bits of it,' Kathy replied honestly. 'I do know that sixteen years ago, around the time my father died, your uncle caused some awful upheaval in my mother's life. She always looked rather sad after that.'

'There are two sides to every story,' murmured Will. 'Are you being hard on him, do you think?'

Kathy shook her head vehemently. 'My mother was the softest, kindest person on this earth. It just couldn't happen that *she* could cause anyone hurt—she hated hurting people.' Her tone was dismissive. 'Anyway, it's my history, not yours.'

He nodded. 'You're right,' he said softly. 'I'm concerned only because it affects you, Kathy. It must have been hard for you when your mother died and you were left to look after Lindy.'

He leaned forward and looked at her seriously for a moment, sweeping her face with those startling blue eyes.

'Forget the past, Kathy. What about the future? What do you want for yourself? A career, a life on the stage, children…?'

Kathy shivered at his close scrutiny. If only my future could include you, she thought wistfully. The previous few minutes had shown only too clearly that he and she had different viewpoints. They could be friends perhaps, but anything more permanent was out of the question—and more and more she was coming to the conclusion that there was something in Will's life that he kept separate.

His smile also had a hint of sadness, and he put up a hand to stroke back the tendrils of hair from her face, running his finger down past her slightly parted lips and across her jaw.

'Don't look so worried,' he murmured. 'Perhaps it's a good thing we can't see too far ahead.'

Tears suddenly prickled at the back of Kathy's eyes. Will might be a Curtis, but his gentle perception of her situation when her mother had died revealed a kindly understanding. Her face flamed and she stood up quickly, embarrassed that he should see what that touch did to her and her emotions.

She started clearing the plates quickly from the makeshift table. 'It's getting quite late. I must get back and do some work in the garden, otherwise it'll defeat me. Everything grows at such a pace, and it'll probably rain soon, making it even more difficult…'

Kathy realised that she was gabbling slightly. Never mind, anything to stop the moment becoming too intimate and revealing feelings for Will she would rather keep buried!

She carried the mound of dishes into the little galley. It was like a child's playhouse, she thought, everything in miniature—no wonder someone the size of Will might find it a little uncomfortable. Suddenly she realised that coming into this small space might have been a mistake. She was intensely aware of Will's large frame with his naked, muscled chest dangerously close to her.

He was standing in the doorway, holding on to the lintel with both arms above his head and gazing down at her with amusement, as if he'd read the reason for her swift departure from the deck.

'Leave those now—I'll do them later,' he murmured. 'You're having a day off today.'

It seemed extremely crowded in the confined space. Will was very, very close to her, and her temperature seemed to have shot up several degrees! It was as if she'd just done two miles on the running machine in the gym. Kathy felt breathless, every sense aware of him. She had a feverish anticipation that something— she couldn't articulate what—was going to happen. There was a short silence between them, and his eyes roamed over her face. Then he stepped forward and lifted her face up to his.

'Have you any idea how beautiful you are, Kathy Macdowell?' he said thickly.

The arc of her thick lashes swept the curve of her cheek as she looked down, confused by her own conflicting emotions and the proximity of his strong body. It was nearly perfect—the day, the place, the man...

Before she could look up again his lips had come down to brush hers with the delicacy of a butterfly's touch. Her heart started thumping like a piston with shock, and she trembled slightly.

'This is a lovely way to end the day, and it's something I've been longing to do,' he whispered.

Then his mouth was over hers again, more demanding, forcefully teasing her lips apart, his finger stroking the length of her neck to the top of her shirt and the cleft of her breasts. For a second she allowed herself to respond—hadn't she dreamt of this since the day she'd first seen Will? Her arms twined about his neck and her body arched against his, feeling the throb of desire crackle between them.

Before she knew what was happening, he had lifted her bodily, without relinquishing her mouth, and laid her gently on a bunk in the barge's little cabin. He lowered his hard male body onto hers and one hand slipped into her blouse and softly caressed her breast, his legs gently easing hers apart. She felt resistance gradually slipping away.

Then suddenly a small voice started to hammer insistently at the back of her head. Don't be a fool, Kathy! Stop this madness before it goes too far! As she felt Will's kisses become more demanding, despair seemed to flood her mind. There were just too many reasons not to continue, but the strongest one was a voice from the past. Her mother's words jumped off the page of the diary even now with vivid warning. 'No matter how he bullies me I will not give in. The Curtises are all the same—they want to own your soul!'

Her mother would have not wanted her to have had anything to do with a Curtis—so she wouldn't.

With every ounce of energy she possessed, Kathy pushed him viciously away, her voice harsh, uncompromising.

'No! We must stop this, Will. We're being utterly foolish, behaving like children!'

He levered himself up and looked down at her, his hair tousled, his forehead puckering in shocked bewilderment.

'What the hell do you mean? Behaving like children? We're two adults, enjoying ourselves!'

Kathy stood up abruptly, pulling her blouse primly back in place. 'Maybe you can make love with no other thought but enjoyment. I need more commitment than that, and there are too many pitfalls…'

Will's eyes narrowed, his expression becoming

flinty. 'You're still thinking of Randolph, aren't you? You can't bloody well separate the two of us. We're not joined at the hip, you know—I do have my own thoughts and ideas. You're letting your opinion of my uncle rule your life!'

Kathy's eyes sparked angrily. 'I let no one rule my life. However, not only do I feel I'm consorting with the enemy when we…do this, but you and I have to work together. We have a professional relationship—perhaps we should keep it like that.'

He caught hold of her shoulders as she brushed past him, and forced her round to look at him. Those deep blue eyes bore into hers.

'The trouble with you, Kathy Macdowell, is that you can't allow yourself to be happy. Don't tell me you didn't enjoy what we were doing—I won't believe you. The truth is, you're obsessed with what you imagine Randolph has done to you—and possibly your mother—to the exclusion of anything else!'

There was a look of sadness in his face, and Kathy's throat constricted. Will was right—she *had* allowed her feelings for his uncle to inhibit her relationship with him—but the past was too strong to ignore.

'I…I hope we can still be…friendly colleagues.' Her voice faltered. 'You see, I didn't come on the barge with this in mind. I'm sorry if I gave you the wrong idea… Do you understand? I should have realised—'

'That I was overstepping the mark?' finished Will harshly. 'No, Kathy, it was my fault. I misjudged you. I thought this was what we both wanted—but I was wrong.'

Kathy's heart thumped. In so many ways she longed to be held in Will's arms—and more! He was the sexiest and most exciting man she'd ever met but, knowing his background, how could she trust him?

She stepped off the barge, her face flushed with embarrassment at the situation, and started to walk home along the canal path, with Rafter trotting at her heels. She didn't look back, but she could feel Will's gaze following her.

Will watched her until she disappeared round a bend and cursed bitterly to himself. Why in heaven's name had he allowed himself to come on so strong? Because he couldn't help it, he reflected gloomily. In a way he had tried to change their relationship by making love to her, but it hadn't worked, he thought savagely.

He gazed unseeingly across the rolling fields. He was sure the attraction wasn't just one-way. He had felt the passion in Kathy's kiss, the way her body had responded to his. His hand clenched on the rail before him. If only things had been different. If only his uncle hadn't had to put his land up for sale, and his father hadn't needed all his support. Kathy had been right when she'd said he had another life beside the front he presented to her.

Angrily, he flung a stick along the tow-path for Magnus to chase, and watched him moodily as he raced towards it. He wouldn't give up yet—he'd make Kathy Macdowell love him, despite the fact she hated his uncle!

CHAPTER SEVEN

'So, you think the centre needs more facilities. It's a bit old-fashioned, is that it?'

Harry looked quizzically at Kathy and Will, seated in front of him in Will's consulting room. Kathy's old partner had come in for a lunchtime meeting. Although he wouldn't be back at work for at least three months, he wanted to see how things were going on without him. He certainly looked much fitter than he'd done in a long time, thought Kathy.

She flicked a glance at Will, hoping that Harry wouldn't notice the cool atmosphere that had developed between the two of them. It had been a difficult week, to say the least. Since the afternoon on the barge he had barely spoken to her. They had maintained a distant politeness, and he had looked worried and preoccupied. Sometimes Kathy thought he was about to say something to her, then he would turn away with a slight shrug and busy himself with paperwork.

And it was all her fault, she thought miserably. Her mind constantly drifted off on how sweet that afternoon should have been, and what a fool she'd been to respond to Will's love-making so eagerly. The trouble was, she conceded wretchedly, when it came to loving Will, she was torn in two! Didn't she have the example of her mother before her—obviously in some way a target of Randolph's bullying? She'd be a fool to get involved with Will after her mother's experience.

She was aware that Harry was waiting for some kind

119

of reaction to his question. Embarrassed, she brushed
a lock of hair out of her eyes and came back to the
matter in hand, trying to put the case to Harry for improving the medical centre.

'It's just that the other medical centres in Bentham
are offering more in the way of ancillary health care,'
she explained carefully. She didn't want him to feel
that now he was out of the way everything was going
to change radically. 'I don't think our medical care is
old-fashioned in the least, but it might give that impression to a patient looking at the place.'

Harry looked round the room with a hint of bewilderment.

'I must say the centre looks completely different in
the short time I've been away—amazing what a lick of
paint can do and some flower tubs at the front! And
now you want to use the empty room for a part-time
physio and chiropodist—there won't be room for me
when I do come back!'

Will was eagerly leaning forward in his chair, his
hair flopping over his forehead. He brushed it away in
a familiar gesture. 'Of course there'll be plenty of
room, Harry, but I think we should take the opportunity
while we've got the builders in the roof to build on
two more rooms at the side. I'm sure we'd get planning
permission. We could do with a better treatment room,
anyway—the practice nurse has to work in a kind of
cubbyhole at the moment.'

Harry sighed and Kathy knew that he felt out of
things and no longer part of the practice. It was going
to be difficult for a conservative older man like him to
come to terms with fresh ideas—he'd only just adjusted
to using computers! She, however, found it increas-
ingly frustrating when she saw other medical centres

in impressive new buildings with many ancillary services to offer. However, she hoped Will in his enthusiasm wouldn't get too carried away—where Harry was concerned, one step at a time was probably a good idea.

Harry was speaking to Will now, and Kathy forced herself to concentrate.

'You've been here a few weeks now—are you enjoying it enough to stay on after the three-month trial?'

There was the shortest of pauses before Will replied, and as Kathy glanced at him his eyes met hers for a fraction of a second.

'I certainly hope so,' he said lightly. 'Of course, it's a two-way thing, isn't it? I've got to please you as well!'

Suddenly Kathy knew without a shadow of a doubt that if things remained as they were between them, Will would leave. How could she blame him? Working with someone he probably thought of as neurotic and obsessed by dislike of his uncle couldn't be easy—no doubt he'd be happier in Africa where he was appreciated by his colleagues.

Harry's shrewd glance took in both of them. 'I haven't heard any complaints from anyone—only praise from the patients I've seen!'

And that's true, acknowledged Kathy to herself. Will was a great general practitioner, exuding confidence and proficiency with a light touch. He was beginning to make a real difference to the way the practice was run, and the patients loved his warm and easy manner.

On a Monday afternoon there was sometimes an extra surgery to cope with the aftermath of the weekend's minor casualties. Today was such a day, and little Billy Corbett was gazing up owlishly at Kathy through round, wire-rimmed glasses. His small seven-year-old face was solemn, only his widened eyes revealing his apprehension. Her heart went out to him—especially when she regarded his mother who, red-faced, untidy and belligerent, glared angrily down at her son.

Kathy knew Mrs Corbett well. She had the kind of draining personality that demanded all one's energies. While normally Kathy relished dealing with the infinite variety of characters she came across in general practice, today, after her awkward week with Will, she felt rather fragile emotionally.

She sighed inwardly. 'You say Billy pushed this bead up his nostril, Mrs Corbett?'

Mrs Corbett nodded. 'I'm fed up with him, I really am, Doctor. He's up to all sorts of scrapes and I can't be watching him all the time—not with the other kids to look after. And you don't expect someone to shove a bead up their nose.' She gave a heavy, hard-done-by sigh. 'He's always been the difficult one...'

She had a whining, high-pitched voice which, Kathy decided, would drive her mad if she had to listen to it often. A plump baby nestled in the woman's arms, and a toddler clung to her skirt.

Kathy bent down beside the scared-looking little boy, and smiled encouragingly at him, trying to stop the woman's complaining flow.

'My, you're a brave boy, Billy,' she said gently. 'It must be very uncomfortable for you. Will you just let me look up your nose with my special torch and I'll see how far the bead has gone up your nostril? How long has it been up there, Mrs Corbett?'

The woman shrugged. 'Search me. It could have been there all morning—he spends hours up in his room, doing God knows what...'

I'm not surprised, thought Kathy grimly. Anything to get away from a mother like that!

The voice droned on monotonously. 'Then he comes down, looking shifty, whining that he's got this bead up his nose, and expects me to work miracles. He's more trouble than all the others put together. Kids! I tell you, Doctor, if I had my time over again, I wouldn't put myself to the trouble. It's nothing but worry and no thanks...'

Kathy looked at the woman's children. They were quiet, solemn, but with a watchful air—and they were beautiful. She sighed. Some people didn't know how lucky they were. One day she would love to have children of her own... Her heart thudded momentarily as she thought of Will, then she checked herself sharply. For heaven's sake, deal with the matter in hand and stop mooning over something you can't ever have!

She peered up Billy's nose and was relieved to see that the bead hadn't actually worked its way too far up. If it had, he'd have had to go to A and E and have it out under anaesthetic. With any luck it could be prised out without too much trouble.

'Billy, I want you to try and do something for me. Can you hold one nostril very tight and then try and blow down the other side? It might come out that way.'

Obediently the little boy did as he was told a few times, but to no effect. His mother sighed heavily.

'If you don't try harder than that,' she threatened, 'you'll get a smack from me you won't forget...'

Kathy saw Billy flinch and swallowed her irritation. She needed to keep the child as calm and relaxed as possible—but the mother seemed bent on terrifying him even more! She patted Billy on the head soothingly, deciding that this might be a good time to call on Will's expertise.

'Don't worry, we'll try another method. I'm going to ask Dr Curtis to come in and help me—he's very good at this sort of thing.' Kathy turned to the child's mother. 'If you'd like to sit in the waiting room with the other children for a while?'

Mrs Corbett looked mulishly from Kathy to her small son. 'Shouldn't I be with him?' she demanded. 'He needs the comfort of his own mother near him.'

Some comfort! Kathy looked at her reflectively. She was the kind of woman who would make an issue out of everything, a drama out of nothing, and she could just imagine her throwing a fit of hysterics as she watched the procedure!

'Billy's a very grown-up little boy,' Kathy said briskly but firmly. 'I would prefer it if you were waiting for him when we've taken the bead out, and then I'm sure he'll need you around.'

She pressed the intercom and asked Ruth to send in Dr Curtis when he was available. Mrs Corbett stood her ground stubbornly.

'I'm not leaving,' she said in a loud, aggressive tone. 'I know my rights and my child's got the right to have me with him.'

Kathy counted to ten—any minute now she was going to tell this woman to go to hell, and frogmarch her out of the room! Billy had been watching the exchange and suddenly started crying with such big hiccupping sobs that his little brother and sister joined in.

'There!' declared Mrs Corbett in tones of satisfaction. 'You've frightened him now—he wants me to stay with him!'

The children's wails became louder and Mrs

Corbett's voice became more belligerent, and as her method of quietening her children seemed to be to shout at them, the situation was getting slightly out of hand.

The door of the room opened and closed, and a deep voice cut like a siren over the noise that the Corbett family were making. Kathy's heart leapt with relief. Professionally at least she had no worries about Will Curtis!

'Now, what's going on here? Who is the patient?'

Will's tall frame seemed to dominate the room, giving him an air of authority. His voice was commanding and demanded attention. Kathy flicked a thankful glance at him and was pleased to see that Mrs Corbett looked startled and visibly taken aback, whilst the children were shocked into silence and watched him with round eyes.

Kathy ushered Billy forward. 'This young man's got a bead stuck up his nose—left nostril. It's only a little way up. He's tried to blow it down, to no avail, so I think we'll try another way. I've asked Mrs Corbett to wait in the waiting room with the other children while we deal with it.'

'I can stay if I want to,' she whined. 'I'm within my rights. My little boy deserves his mum when he's got to have a horrible thing done to him!'

Will's eyes met Kathy's in a look that said, We've got a right one here! Then he turned to the sour-looking woman.

'Mrs Corbett, I know you want what's best for Billy—and, incidentally, he's not going to have anything horrible done to him—but we must do it our way and we can't have the distraction of other children making noise here. I'm sure you'll understand. Billy seems very grown-up to me—you don't mind your mum and brother and sister waiting outside, do you?'

He gave a friendly wink to the little boy.

Mrs Corbett opened her mouth to protest again, looked at Will's flinty expression, then gathered herself and stomped out of the room with her other children, grumbling loudly. Mentally Kathy gave three cheers and thanked God that Will had turned up at the right moment! He had used exactly the right manner with someone as awkward as Mrs Corbett, who responded to polite authority. It was at times like these that Kathy realised how irreplaceable Will was to the practice— and how she'd miss him if he left.

He turned to Billy, now quiet but looking rather forlorn. He bent down to the child's level and put an arm round his waist.

'Now, Billy, do you like cars?'

Billy nodded wordlessly.

'I've got a very special car to show you when I've got this bead out of your nose. It's got lots of little tricks and I think you'll find it very funny. You think about that car while I'm looking at your nose. I'll squirt some of this special liquid up your nostril so that you won't feel me prodding around so much—but the stiller you are, the quicker I'll be!'

He looked up at Kathy. 'This Xylocaine should constrict the mucous membrane as well, reduce the swelling.'

He quickly sprayed some local anaesthetic around the trapped bead, and Kathy held Billy's head still. She watched Will's bent head as he peered up the offending nostril, talking soothingly to his young patient all the time. Soft, dark hair curled over the nape of Will's neck and she felt a great temptation to reach out and touch it. Only days ago her arms had been entwined around that neck, her fingers threaded through his thick hair… She snapped herself angrily back to attention, forcing herself to concentrate on the matter in hand.

Will was now probing with the nasal forceps to dislodge the bead, and the child squirmed uncomfortably.

'Steady, Billy, you're doing so well. I think he's the bravest man we've had in here this morning, isn't he, Dr Macdowell? Just hold on for a second more and I think we'll have that old bead in our grasp… Yes, here it comes—hurray!'

With an air of triumph he held up the small blue bead that had caused the trouble. Billy looked at it, round-eyed, and touched his nose cautiously. Will smiled down at him.

'You're a very brave boy, but I want you to promise me that you won't go shoving beads up your nose again. It's *not* a good idea! It might not be so easy to get out next time.'

He delved into his pocket and brought out a small tin car, which he wound up and put on the floor. The toy whizzed all over the carpet, and every time it hit a piece of furniture it turned rapidly in the opposite direction, flashing lights and emitting a little whistle.

Billy watched it silently for a minute, then a big smile spread over his solemn little face. Will picked up the toy and handed it to the child.

'There you are, Billy. It's yours for being so brave.'

The child looked at it unbelievingly for a moment, then he looked up at Will and Kathy through his round, slightly crooked glasses.

'For me?' he asked incredulously, his ordeal with the bead forgotten completely. 'Thank you very much!'

He had a gruff, deep little voice that tugged at

Kathy's heartstrings. Despite his mother, he seemed to have picked up some good manners from somewhere. Her eyes met Will's over the child's head—there were some patients who were lovable despite their parents!

Kathy took the child to his mother in the waiting room. She grabbed his hand and marched out without saying a word. At the door, Billy turned round and gave a little wave. Kathy smiled at him and then went over to Ruth behind the desk in Reception.

'Could you get me Mrs Layton's blood results, Ruth? I think we should have them by now and she has an appointment this afternoon.' She spoke rather apprehensively. Monday wasn't Ruth's best time and she was liable to be even more prickly than usual.

'Of course, Dr Macdowell, I'll bring them to you straight away.'

Kathy blinked. Ruth's voice had sounded almost cheery, quite unlike her usual doleful tones! She looked at the receptionist more closely—was this really Ruth? She hadn't had time to observe her that morning, but her hair seemed quite different from the severe bun she usually wore, scraped tightly back from her face. It had been cut into a short bob, and the dreary brown cardigan and skirt had been replaced by a flower-printed dress.

'Nice day, isn't it?' Ruth said pleasantly. 'Would you like some tea now?'

Kathy tried not to look too astonished. 'Er, yes, that would be nice, Ruth, if it's not too much trouble...'

'No, no, I'll bring it in with the blood results.'

Kathy watched Ruth's stocky little figure walk briskly out to the kitchen, and she shook her head in bafflement. She wasn't sure, but she could have sworn that the receptionist had given a half-smile as she'd gone out! Perhaps she'd won some money in the lottery! Kathy shook her head helplessly and went back to her room. Will was still there, propping himself up on her desk and running his eye over one of the many medical journals that came every week.

He looked up as she entered. 'Returned our young hero to his devoted mother?' he enquired.

Kathy nodded with a rueful smile. 'Not a word of thanks from her ladyship. Bad luck, being landed with a mother like that. You did marvellously to keep that little boy calm. I was very impressed with the all-dancing car!'

Will grinned. 'I bought a job lot from a street trader in London,' he said. 'The only thing is, they're so popular I'm afraid young patients may try and come to the doctor's even when they're well!'

'I don't think young Master Corbett has had much kindness in his life somehow—his mother may love him, but she has a funny way of showing it. Some children do 'ave 'em, as the saying goes!'

Their eyes met in mutual understanding and sympathy for the child, and suddenly Kathy felt a relaxation of the atmosphere that had built up between them during the past week. Out of hours their relationship may have hit the rocks, but thankfully they could still work together. It was as if a barrier of awkwardness had melted, and Kathy conceded that sometimes patients could act as go-betweens—she even felt a flicker of gratitude towards the annoying Mrs Corbett!

There was a knock at the door, and Ruth marched in with two cups of tea on a tray.

'Here's the tea and the blood results you wanted, Dr Kathy. I'm afraid you've both got rather a full house today.'

She swept out and Will looked after her, an astonished expression on his face.

'Am I dreaming, or was that Ruth that just came in?'
he asked incredulously. 'She looks quite different.
What the hell's happened to her?'

Kathy looked at his mystified face and giggled. 'She
seems to have had a complete make-over,' she said,
and then, without thinking, added, 'Perhaps she's in
love!'

'Ah, yes,' agreed Will. 'It must be spring fever—
makes people do odd things. Talking of which...' He
looked at her quizzically. 'I haven't seen you alone for
a while—not since our afternoon on the barge. Perhaps
we still have things to talk about.'

Kathy blushed. Why did the man have to bring that
up? Then she thought, Why shouldn't he? Why have
any embarrassment between us when we should at the
least be amicable colleagues? She looked at him can-
didly and took a deep breath.

'Will, the picnic was lovely—you went to so much
trouble. Lindy and I enjoyed it so much. I'm sorry it
had to end on an awkward note. I should have realised—'

'That I'd want my wicked way with you?' An impish
grin lit his face, then Will shook his head wryly. 'No,
Kathy, it was my fault. I got the wrong idea. But it
was inexcusable to pounce on you like that. Probably
too much wine...'

'You and me both!' she said lightly, and blushed.
Was he gently hinting that she had led him on—and
wasn't there a grain of truth in that?

His eyes held hers for a moment and she felt a familiar flutter of her heart, perhaps mixed with relief
that they could at least still work together.

'Then let's put it behind us and start afresh,' he said gently. 'Actually, I've a favour to ask you, Kathy—if it's possible.'

Kathy looked at him warily, and he gave a rueful smile.

'Don't worry, it's nothing that involves picnics on barges, or heavy-handed doctors. Lindy did mention that your cousin was thinking of letting the farm—I really am interested. The barge seems to be getting smaller, or I'm getting bigger. I'm desperate to move and I wondered if you'd introduce me to your cousin so that I can talk the thing over? If you've time after work this week, I'd really appreciate it as I have rather a lot on in the next month.'

Kathy gave an inward sigh. She felt that the less Will and she saw each other out of working hours, the better! On the other hand, she wondered if his comments on having a lot on in the next few weeks were to re-assure her that there'd be no chance for them to spend time together, anyway!

'You think your father will be joining you soon, then?'

He looked at her guardedly, and once more she was aware of that mysterious other life of his which he kept so carefully apart.

'It could be… I have every hope. However, whether he comes or not, I shall have to move out of the barge soon before I'm crippled!'

Kathy nodded. 'Fine—I'll take you there later. Perhaps John would be intrigued to swop lifestyles with you!'

She shuffled the papers on her desk rather pointedly. 'Was there anything else I could help you with before I start?'

Will looked more serious and nodded. 'I wanted to ask if you'll be seeing Gary Layton's mother. I think you said she was having treatment of some kind?'

Kathy pointed to the paper on her desk. 'Seeing her today as a matter of fact—these are the results of her blood tests. Any reason?'

'If she reveals that she knows about her son's problem, it might be a help—or any background information. I'm seeing Gary later today for a check-up. He's now on rehab and hopefully has stuck to the regime. I just hope he turns up.'

Kathy smiled reassuringly across at Pat Layton's exhausted-looking face. She wondered if the woman had any inkling about her son's drug habit. She couldn't tell her because the boy was no longer a minor, but she hated the thought of the poor woman being in ignorance of the facts. She looked down at the blood-test results. Pat had iron-deficiency anaemia. Her haemoglobin was less than 10 grammes—no wonder she was feeling so desperately tired. The anaemia could have several underlying causes, which would have to be ascertained with a series of tests.

'I'm glad you came to see me, Mrs Layton. It's always a good thing to get yourself checked if you're worried, and from your tests we can see that you have iron-deficiency anaemia—that's why you're feeling so tired. We need to know why you are iron deficient—I'm going to refer you for a gastroscopy and we'll go from there. It's probably just some inflammation in your gullet, possibly exacerbated by stress. I'd also like you to have an endoscopy to check out your indigestion.'

Pat looked alarmed, but Kathy said soothingly with

an encouraging smile, 'These things sound rather drastic, but I assure you it won't be too awful. You'll have a sedative drug when the tube is introduced, and similarly with the endoscope. We'll be able to see if you have an ulcer or any inflammation and give you the right treatment.'

Pat sighed with a defeated air and gave a faint smile. 'It sounds rather frightening, Doctor, but I guess it's as well to know what's going on.'

She hesitated for a second and bit her lip as if she had something else to say, then suddenly her face crumpled and she put her hands to her face.

Kathy leaned forward anxiously. 'What is it, Mrs Layton? You know this procedure is nothing to worry about, and only takes a short time. If it is an ulcer that's causing the problem we have very good drugs nowadays. Soon you'll probably be feeling as right as rain...'

A muffled sob came from behind the woman's hands. Kathy caught the words 'sorry' and 'I can't keep it to myself'.

She went round the desk and put her arm around Pat's shoulders. 'What is it?' she asked gently. 'Do you feel you could tell me about it?'

The woman gave a watery smile and blew her nose hard. 'It...it's ridiculous,' she gulped, 'but it's been preying on my mind ever since the day my mother's handbag was snatched.'

'What's been worrying you?'

Pat gave a mirthless laugh. 'As a magistrate, I sit in court and sometimes wonder how people let their lives get into such a mess. Now I can appreciate their difficulties! You see, you never think these kinds of things can happen to you.'

The patient shrugged helplessly.

'I've been guilty of withholding information,' she said sadly.

For a minute Kathy wondered if she had learnt about her son's drug problem, but she kept quiet, letting Pat tell her own story.

'You see, I think I know who was involved in attacking my mother—but I couldn't bring myself to tell the police.'

'Why on earth not?' Kathy felt baffled. Surely if she had an inkling who had attacked her own mother, Pat should have given that information?

The woman's shoulders dropped and she whispered, 'Because…because I think it was my own son who was standing by the door as the lookout! He…he was part of the wretched gang!'

Kathy was silent for a second, a jolt of horror running through her. No wonder the woman had looked so terrible when she'd brought in her mother for treatment after the attack! The shock must have been profound and, of course, it could all be tied up with the boy's need to get money to feed his drug habit.

Kathy went back to her chair and sat down. 'Have you tackled your son about this?'

Pat shook her head. 'I couldn't bring myself to do it. He's been acting very aggressively recently—quite out of character.'

'What do you think has changed him?'

The woman paused for a second, then said with obvious difficulty, 'I'm afraid my husband left me for a much younger woman about a year ago. It wasn't really such a surprise as we hadn't had a very happy married life for some years, but I think it was when Laurence left that Gary changed. He adores his father and he probably thought he'd abandoned us all.'

Which he had, reflected Kathy grimly. She looked sympathetically at her patient. She couldn't discount the possibility that her patient's medical problems *were* stress-related. Life for Pat had become a series of shocks, but she had to speak to her son.

Kathy spoke gently to the sad-looking woman.

'The only way forward is to let Gary know that you are aware he was involved in the attack on his grandmother. He may be carrying as big a burden of guilt as you are. Perhaps at the time he didn't even realise it was his own grandmother. Whatever, you must try and persuade him to go to the police.'

'I know you're right,' acknowledged Pat. 'I suppose I bottled it up because I couldn't bring myself to admit to anyone that Gary could do such a thing. I've just got to get on with it, though.' She smiled warily at Kathy. 'Thanks for listening to me—and for the advice. I do feel better for telling you.'

She walked to the door. Kathy followed her and squeezed her arm comfortingly. 'Let me know how you get on regarding your son—and remember I'll be sending you for tests soon, and I want you to take the iron tablets I've prescribed. Make another appointment to see me next week.'

Kathy puffed out her cheeks in amazement. People's lives never ceased to amaze her. That, of course, was part of the fascination of the job—the infinite variety of things that happened within a family. She felt acutely sorry for Pat—everything seemed to be crashing around her. She'd done a lot for the community and anything that went wrong in her life would attract a lot of interest. Sadly she reflected that Pat was probably in for more shocks regarding her son—perhaps he would feel able to confide in his mother eventually.

Kathy pressed the intercom to Will's room. 'Dr Curtis, when you're free, I'd like a word.'

'So that's it. Pat Layton's been keeping the secret of Gary's involvement of the handbag snatch to herself—but I don't think she has a clue he's doing drugs.'

Will nodded thoughtfully. 'Could explain why he got mixed up with the robbery. It also might be the background to him wanting to change his habits. I bet he didn't realise that it was his own grandmother that was getting mugged until afterwards. Could have jolted him into action, do you think?'

'What a mess,' sighed Kathy. 'But you're right— perhaps Gary really does want to get off drugs. His mother is going to try and persuade him to give himself up to the police on the handbag snatch episode.'

'And I have hopes that Gary will stick to the programme. At least he did turn up today, and his urine test was OK—it showed he hadn't done heroin in the past week. We'll keep our fingers crossed.'

A long afternoon came to an end and Kathy finished with a sigh of satisfaction, calling out goodbye to Ruth who was on the phone.

Will was standing by his car in the car park.

'Is there any chance you can take me to your cousin now?' he asked. 'The next few days are going to be a bit hectic—I'd really appreciate it.'

Kathy sighed, thinking of hot baths and an uninterrupted evening in. Then she relented, conceding that at least it would get the visit over with. She was also slightly worried about John as she hadn't heard from him since her visit. He had promised to ring her with his decision about leaving the farm, and perhaps Will's suggestion would help him make up his mind.

With relief, Kathy thought John looked much better. His rough stubble had been shaved, and he was busy rebuilding a dry-stone wall round the house. He looked up as Will drove in, and smiled when he realised that Kathy was with him.

'Have you had any thoughts about our conversation the other day?' she asked him as she got out of the car.

He grinned, tipping his hat to the back of his head and looking quite light-hearted.

'Thought of nothing else,' he admitted. 'It was a wonderful idea of yours. It's given me a new lease of life. I can't think of anything better than taking a year or two off from this place. I'm going to the estate agents tomorrow—they can let it for me.'

'Perhaps I can save you the trouble,' said Kathy with a smile. 'This is Will Curtis, who's joined me at the practice. He's looking for somewhere to rent.'

John Macdowell looked at Will narrowly. 'Randolph's nephew, I take it?' he growled. Then he shrugged and chuckled. 'Perhaps I should be grateful to the old bastard. If this land issue hadn't come up I might not have thought of changing direction.'

The two men shook hands amiably enough. 'If you get an assessment from the agents and an idea of what you want to charge, perhaps we could go ahead,' suggested Will, adding with a twinkle, 'If you want to swop your house for the barge I'm renting and go round England in it, you're very welcome. I know my friend is only too willing to rent it out again!'

John grinned. 'Thanks, but, no, thanks! I'm off to see the world, I've decided—America, Australia,

Africa. Bentham's getting too small for me! The world's my oyster... Now, if you'll follow me, I'll show you over the place. It is a little run-down, but I believe you're the sort that likes doing places up...'

They followed him into the house.

'What did you think of it?' asked Kathy as they drove back to the surgery to pick up her car.

'Absolutely perfect! I love the position, and there are plenty of rooms to spread myself about. And if my father comes, I know it'll suit him—all that space for him to relax in. I'm grateful to you for taking me, Kathy.'

He shot a speculative look across at Kathy. 'By the way, I've been meaning to discuss something with you for some time, but there's never been the opportunity...'

Because we hadn't been talking to each other, thought Kathy wryly, remembering their awkward silences at lunchtime recently.

'It's...well, rather complicated, and might take some time. It's something I've found out, and it's been preying on my mind that it's something you ought to know.'

'What on earth do you mean?' Kathy frowned, but she was intrigued. 'Why can't you tell me now? I don't like mysteries and, anyway, what's the point of referring to it if we can't discuss it?'

Will sighed. 'This won't be easy—I'd rather make an appointment with you. The car's not the right place.'

Kathy shrugged. 'It all sounds rather formal, but if you want to that's OK.'

Will turned into the surgery car park and drew up beside Kathy's car. The surgery was closed now, and everything was shut up. He looked up at the building with a smile of satisfaction.

'Beginning to look a bit sprucer now—the hanging baskets look very cheery. Perhaps we can have some clematis climbing up that wall.' Then he frowned, peering up at a side window. 'That's strange,' he muttered. 'I see the light's been left on in my surgery. There's a time switch on it—it can't go on without being over-ridden. I think I'll just go and check inside. It could be the builders, but usually they're very meticulous.'

Kathy put a hand on his arm as he opened the door. 'Be careful, Will—it could be an intruder.'

Will grimaced. 'If there's anyone there I'm going to get the bastards,' he growled. 'Stay out of the way, Kathy, just in case.'

He walked quietly over to the main door, opening it gently with his key. Kathy followed him—she wasn't going to be left out of the action if there was any!

There was silence for a minute, then a shout, and Kathy jumped as she heard Will's voice yelling.

'You little toe-rag! You've cheated everyone, haven't you? Now I think you're going to have to account for yourself!'

The sound of something crashing to the ground prompted Kathy to dash through the door, her heart pounding. As if in a still photograph, she saw Will lying on the ground, a tall bookcase toppled over beside him. Standing frozen to the spot, looking down at Will, was a panic-stricken youth, clutching a small package. It was Gary Layton.

CHAPTER EIGHT

FOR a second nobody moved, and Kathy stared, horrified, at Will's prone figure. What the hell had happened? Had Gary attacked Will, or had the bookcase fallen on him in a struggle? A mixed feeling of fury and bewilderment engulfed her. The whole thing seemed to have happened as quickly as a bolt of lightning.

Gulping down her rising panic and trying to behave objectively and professionally, Kathy stumbled to Will's side and dropped down beside him. She put a finger on his carotid artery, and laid her head on his chest to listen to his heart. Oh, God—let him be all right!

His eyes flew open, and he gazed up at her with a mischievous grin.

'I think I need the kiss of life very urgently,' he murmured.

A wave of relief swept through her, and she fought back tears, before croaking hoarsely, 'Thank the Lord you're OK. You gave me a horrible fright! Don't move!'

'Don't fuss,' he growled tersely, giving a passable imitation of his uncle. 'I'll live—just a bump, that's all.'

He gave a grimace of pain and sat up, gingerly feeling a rapidly swelling bruise above his eyes where the corner of the bookcase had caught him.

'Bloody hell,' he murmured. 'I've heard of seeing

stars, but this is ridiculous! Luckily it was just wood on wood!'

Kathy suddenly remembered the reason they were there, and looked up sharply at Gary, who seemed completely paralysed with shock. He was gazing mutely at Will, his face as white as a sheet, and all at once some inner control seemed to snap inside Kathy.

How dared this youth abuse his doctor's trust and break into the surgery, no doubt helping himself to any drugs that were in the building? A picture of his mother's anguished expression and his grandmother's shocked face after her mugging flashed into Kathy's mind, and her blood boiled with fury at the further pain he was going to cause them.

Gary saw her staring at him and was abruptly galvanised into action, turning to run towards the entrance. With a cry of rage Kathy launched herself at the startled boy and pushed him as hard as she could to the ground. She was a tall, strong girl and he wasn't expecting such power. He staggered back, shaken, and lay dazed for a second beside Will, then tried to lever himself up.

'Oh, no, you don't, my lad,' Kathy said grimly. 'You're staying put!'

She held his neck in a vice-like grip, fury lending her added strength. 'Just what the hell do you think you're doing, you little idiot,' she grunted. 'If you've harmed a hair of Dr Curtis's head you'll be up for grievous bodily harm—that's a promise!'

Gary squirmed, flailing his arms to remove the pressure from his neck. 'I didn't hurt him,' he gasped. 'Honest. The bookcase fell over when I was running away.'

'And did you find any drugs worth selling on, Gary,

or were they for your own consumption? You've sunk pretty low to be stealing from the surgery, haven't you?'

'I didn't mean to hurt anyone,' he whined.

Kathy tightened her grip on him. 'They're going to throw the book at you. What a nice thing to tell your mother…'

'He's not a very nice lad.'

Will stood up and looked down with scorn at the boy. 'Nice one, Gary,' he grated. 'Did you think stealing drugs was part of the rehab programme?'

Gary suddenly began to whimper. 'I didn't mean any harm, honest. And I didn't pull the bookcase on top of the doctor. I only came in to get something to put me on…'

'To sell, you mean. I know you were getting enough for your own needs—thirty mils twice a day from a daily prescription, wasn't it? I take it you owe a bit of money, Gary, and this is the easy way to get it?'

Will's face was as hard as stone, his purple bruise giving him a rather sinister air. 'How the hell did you get yourself into this mess, you stupid fool?'

He bent down and prised away the package still clutched in the boy's hand. 'As I thought,' he remarked grimly. 'Five ten-milligram ampoules of diamorphine. This is kept for emergencies, people who might be having a heart attack and in excruciating pain—not some little pain in the arse who's been mixing with the wrong sort of people. Did it take you long to break open the cupboard?'

'I'm sorry… I won't do it again. Please, give us a chance.'

The boy looked up at them with stricken eyes, and Kathy released him reluctantly. 'You've had your chance, Gary,' she said coldly. 'And do you mind telling us what mean, sneaky little method you used to get into the surgery? Why didn't the alarm go off?'

'I…I stayed in a cupboard after seeing Dr Curtis this afternoon, and I just turned the alarm off when the receptionist left. I *am* sorry,' he burst out suddenly, tears running down his face. 'I've been worse than you think, anyway. Done really bad things, so what does it matter? I'll be put in jail probably.'

Kathy looked at Will and grimaced. 'I think it would be interesting to know what Gary's talking about, don't you?' she said meaningly.

Will nodded. 'Dr Macdowell's right. If you're hiding anything at all, now is the time to tell us. You'll have to tell the police, anyway, in a few minutes.'

He took the boy's shoulder and led him firmly through to his surgery, pushing Gary into a chair and locking the door behind them all. He folded his arms and stood forbiddingly in front of the trembling youth.

'Right, spill the beans, Gary. Just what is behind all this stupidity?'

Kathy could almost feel sorry for the boy. He looked pathetic, sitting huddled in the chair, his head in his hands. Then he looked up at them rather hopelessly.

'I got in with the wrong lot at school,' he began slowly. 'Home was a bit bleak at the time—Dad left us, and Mum was very busy with her councillor and magistrate things.'

'So that's your excuse, eh? No loving home life?' Will's voice was hard.

The boy squirmed uncomfortably. 'I was no good at games, see, and work was dead boring. With these lads I belonged to a group, and their parties were good fun…'

'Plenty of booze and drugs, I suppose?'

'We started off with a bit of grass,' admitted the youth, 'then it sort of got out of hand. I found myself owing money for stronger stuff.'

He paused, as if gathering his resources. Kathy and Will said nothing, waiting for him to finish.

Suddenly Gary buried his head in his hands again and in a muffled choked voice blurted, 'I've been really stupid. One of them said it would be dead easy to get ready cash. Just follow some old biddy who'd been to get her pension and do a bag snatch.'

'So you joined in with the idea?' Will's voice was low and hard.

Gary looked up; his eyes were red-rimmed. 'Yeah, I didn't want to, but I said I'd be lookout. They did it in the supermarket and I didn't see who they'd done.' His voice faltered. 'Afterwards I learnt it was my own gran. I felt really bad, and that's when I decided I had to try and get off the stuff. I do want to, honest...'

'But you've still got people to pay off—is that it?'

'Yes,' he whispered. 'I...I'm sorry.'

Will put a hand on the boy's shoulder and said more gently, 'You've got to be strong now, Gary. You must tell the police what you've told us and take your punishment—then you can start again. If your mum and gran know how sorry you are, I'm sure they'll be shocked—but they'll forgive you.'

'You know, I feel almost relieved about all of this,' confided Kathy to Will, as an hour later they left the police station, having given statements and tried to comfort Gary's mother who had arrived in a state of shock and horror at the news of her son's actions.

'Yes, it's all come out, and hopefully the boy will

get sorted.' Will chuckled. 'Mind you, I think the lad's had a good part of his punishment! I don't think he expected the half nelson you inflicted on him—very impressive! All this working out in the gym hasn't been in vain. I'm glad you were on my side!'

'I certainly enjoyed that bit of it,' said Kathy with relish, then added with a sigh, 'Sometimes there are advantages to being a big girl!'

He grinned. 'I see a fine, athletic figure,' he commented lightly, his eyes travelling appreciatively over her tall frame.

Kathy shuddered. 'You mean enormous!' she protested.

'I mean superb!' Will corrected firmly. 'However, we can't always rely on your attacking skills to keep intruders at bay in the surgery. That burglar alarm needs updating. If even a little squirt like Gary Layton can immobilise it, then it's useless! Of course, it will be another thing for poor old Harry to get used to!'

He flicked a glance at his watch. 'Look, Kathy, I don't know about you but I'm starving. I'd have had something to eat an hour ago but for this little excursion to the police station. Why don't we go to that Italian restaurant near the surgery, and I can tell you what I've been wanting to talk to you about?'

'Oh, Will, I really couldn't face going out now...'

'You've got to eat,' he said reasonably.

Kathy hesitated. She wanted to hear what Will had to say. It sounded intriguing, but the Italian place was small and stuffy, and usually very noisy. After the alarms of the evening she felt like being quiet. Asking him back to the cottage might be rather foolhardy— after all, did she really want to be alone with Will after their afternoon on the barge? She knew Lindy would be away for the night with a friend.

At last she said reluctantly, 'Why don't you get a take-away? I'll go home now and put some plates in the oven—you come on with the food.'

He smiled, a rather relieved smile, she thought, as if he had been expecting a flat refusal.

'See you in a minute,' he murmured.

Kathy pushed her plate away and leaned back in her chair. The food had been unexpectedly tasty, and they had talked for some time about security at the surgery and the various changes they might make to the building. Will had insisted on making the coffee, and put a cup down beside her.

She took a sip and looked up at him expectantly. 'Well, you said you had something to talk to me about—what was it?'

Will gave a half-laugh, running an agitated hand through his hair. 'This isn't going to be very easy,' he admitted slowly.

Kathy stared at him in a baffled way. 'What do you mean? Is it bad news?'

He smiled wryly. 'Depends on your point of view. You see, I've been trying to clear up a mystery—but the answer will come as even more of a shock to you than it did to me!'

'For goodness' sake!' With a sigh of impatience Kathy jumped up from her chair and looked at him with a puzzled smile. 'Stop beating about the bush— what *is* this extraordinary mystery?'

'It's something I feel you have a right to know— and also I think it will explain a few things about my uncle.'

There was something grave about his tone that made Kathy's heart thump uncomfortably, and the smile died from her lips.

'It…it sounds very serious.'

He walked over to her and put his hands on her shoulders, looking intently down at her face with those fascinating blue eyes.

'When we had our…discussion on the barge the other day,' he began slowly, 'one of the things you mentioned was that Randolph had once hurt your mother very badly. You admitted that was part of your reason for disliking him.'

Involuntarily, his hands gripped her shoulders more tightly. 'Kathy, I don't want anything to come between us. I want us to be friends, good friends, and I know we can be. That's why I wanted to find out about what happened between your mother and my uncle—I needed to try and prove to you that Randolph Curtis isn't the ogre he seems.'

Kathy's large eyes gazed at him in puzzlement. 'I don't understand. Are you telling me you've found out *how* he hurt my mother?'

There was a second's silence, then Will took her hands and said very gently, 'It might possibly have been the other way round, you know.'

Kathy opened her mouth to interrupt, but he put a finger on her lips.

'Kathy, darling, let me finish. I think that the one who was hurt could have been Randolph himself! I think he's carried a burden of grief through the years without being able to unload it.'

'Wh-what on earth do you mean? What are you getting at?'

Through Kathy's fog of bewilderment she heard a

new tenderness in Will's voice, a vague awareness that
he had called her 'darling' and the knowledge that he
was trying very hard to break some extraordinary news
to her as gently as he could.

He sat down beside her.

'Your father died a few months before Lindy was
born, about sixteen years ago, I believe. I think I'm
right in saying that he'd had a long illness. It must have
been incredibly difficult for your mother at that time.'

'Yes…that's true. Lindy never knew him.' Kathy
felt breathless, she could hardly get the words out.

'You see, I wanted to find out how Randolph could
possibly have hurt your mother and, risking your anger,
I asked him!'

Kathy licked dry lips. 'And?' she croaked.

Will's eyes never left her face. 'He told me that
Lindy is his daughter!'

Kathy gazed at Will completely uncomprehendingly
for a moment.

'What the hell are you talking about?' she whispered
slowly at last. 'I refuse to believe it—it's a complete
and utter fabrication. My mother and Randolph Curtis?
Don't make me laugh!'

Her scornful emerald eyes glinted furiously at Will.
'I thought you had something constructive to say about
what had happened between them. If you think a cock
and bull story like that will make me admire Randolph,
you've got another think coming!'

She turned her back on Will and strode off into the
kitchen with her coffee-cup. She hurled it furiously into
the sink, where it shattered noisily. How *dared* he imply that her mother and that…that man had got together? It was outrageous!

Kathy felt tears of anger and horror well up in her

eyes, and she gripped the side of the sink convulsively as the full implication of what Will had said sank in. How could Will imagine that she would think well of his uncle after this information?

'Kathy...Kathy, you have to believe me. I *know* that Randolph was telling me the truth.'

She whirled round to face Will. He was standing just behind her, his expression full of gentle compassion.

'How could you tell he was telling the truth?' she grated scornfully.

'I could tell from his eyes, his voice, his manner, that this was something he had been longing to reveal for many years. He talked for an hour about it, as if the dam gates had released a flood, and I knew with no doubt whatsoever that he was being completely honest.'

Kathy's heart hammered uncomfortably in her chest, then she sprang away from him with a harsh cry.

'No! No, I don't believe this. My mother and Randolph? It's just not possible...is it?' She looked painfully across at Will. 'It can't be true,' she added with more spirit. 'Why would she do anything like that? She loved my father—they had a very happy marriage.'

'I'm sure she did—but think about it. For some years she had looked after a very ill man. She had a child and probably felt lonely, unable to confide her worries to anyone. Along comes someone who falls in love with her—is prepared to comfort her, support her in many ways. You can't blame a lonely, frightened young woman for turning to a man who wants to look after her.'

Kathy shook her head in bewilderment. 'But she never told anybody—and there was her diary. I saw a few lines from an entry she made, and I can never ever forget them. Part of the entry said, ''I will not let Randolph Curtis force me to be under an obligation to him...no matter how he bullies me, I will not give in! The Curtises are all the same—they want to own your soul!'' Doesn't that sound like coercion to you?'

Will sighed. 'From what my uncle told me, your mother was filled with remorse and guilt when she found she was expecting Lindy. She felt she had betrayed the memory of her husband, having an affair while he was alive. Randolph begged her to marry him, or at least to acknowledge that he was Lindy's father. When he realised how devastated your mother felt over the whole thing, he promised her eventually that he would leave her alone. She absolutely refused any monetary or other help from him. She said he was trying to own her when she'd really belonged to her first husband.'

'Then why has he told you now?'

Will stepped towards Kathy and put his hands on her shoulders.

'Put yourself in his place—a man who had to watch the woman he loved bring up their child without an acknowledgement that he was the father. He loved your mother, Kathy, and he didn't want to make her more unhappy after the death of your father, but for all these years he has longed to put things right, as he sees it. He's a lonely man and he thinks that Lindy should know that her father is really alive, and now that your mother has died does it matter?'

He tilted her head towards his and looked at her searchingly. 'Surely you can sympathise with that?'

Kathy gazed at a photo of her mother and father on the mantelpiece. They looked very young and happy, with no hint of the shadows that would overtake their lives later. She conceded to herself that Randolph had put her mother's peace of mind before his own happiness by keeping his paternity of Lindy quiet.

Was there just a chance that, after all, she'd been wrong about his treatment of her mother? Perhaps he wasn't *all* bad... She thought of Lindy going to the stables so happily, enjoying her work, and how she had often remarked about Randolph's kindness towards her, the extra money he would hand her for doing small jobs...

It was a bewildering scenario, and suddenly tears began to stream down Kathy's face. She had loved her mother deeply and the thought of the torment she must have gone through was very painful. She laid her head on Will's shoulder and cried her heart out. He stood against her like a rock and stroked her hair gently.

'It's all right, my darling, don't worry. Everything will turn out for the best. And, if you're honest, if it were you and not Lindy, I'm sure you would want your father to acknowledge you, to tell you he loved you.'

Kathy pulled back from him for a moment and took a handkerchief out of his top pocket, dabbing her eyes with it. 'I...I suppose,' she whispered. 'It's just come as such a bombshell. I find it so hard to believe—that a man I disliked could be Lindy's father.' She looked up at Will. 'How can I tell her?' she said helplessly. 'When's the right time?'

'We'll find the right time,' he said firmly. He held her away from him for a second. 'Randolph has suppressed his longing to tell the world about Lindy. Can you find it in your heart to think differently about him?'

Kathy sighed. 'I don't know what to think, really. I love Lindy very dearly and we're very close. To find out that Randolph Curtis is virtually related to me is, to say the least, a big shock, but I want to do the best for my kid sister. I really do…'

'Of course you do,' said Will gently. 'You've done so well for her, anyway.' He smiled wryly at her. 'So, do you think it's possible that my illustrious relative isn't all bad, that he actually might have some kindly traits?'

Kathy gave a watery smile. 'I could have been wrong, I suppose, but that's not to say I'm with him on the land deal. I suppose you're going to tell me next that he's selling that off for some incredibly kind reason?'

With a flash of intuition Kathy saw to her astonishment that somehow her remark had hit home. A dull flush spread up over Will's strong face.

'Something like that,' he muttered. 'Don't take everything at face value.'

Kathy was silent. She knew better now than to pursue that particular subject, but it was another reminder of the life that he kept apart from her.

'I have to go.' Will picked up his jacket from a chair and smiled ruefully at her. 'I hope all this hasn't bowled you over too much. As I said, I told you with the best of intentions. Not a word will pass Randolph's lips until you decide to tell Lindy—and I hope you will.'

'I suppose I'll have to,' sighed Kathy, 'but I'll pick the time.'

Will looked at her forlorn face. She'd had a bewildering shock that evening and had coped with it remarkably well. He couldn't help himself—he strode forward and took her in his arms again, kissing her lips gently.

'You're so brave,' he murmured. 'I know this has changed your life, but I'll be here for you if you need me.'

His next kiss was more insistent, fiercer, against her warm, soft mouth, then with a barely audible groan he stepped back, forcing himself to be restrained. If he wasn't careful he'd repeat the episode on the barge!

Holding her eyes with his, he said thickly, 'I'll see you soon, Kathy. As I said, I'll be busy after work for the next week or two. I have a commitment that will be demanding a lot of my attention. Leave any messages on the machine.'

He gave a half-wave and let himself out of the front door.

Kathy watched him go, touching her lips where his had been. She felt their imprint still. Then she sat down abruptly on the sofa and buried her head in her hands. It was hard to take in such shattering news all at once. Could it really be true that her mother had had an affair with Randolph Curtis all those years ago? She began to mull over it slowly, recalling every word that Will had said.

Somehow everything began to make sense. A lonely young woman, coping with a very ill husband and not much money. Randolph, with his wealth, status and flattering affection for her, would have seemed an attractive haven. Kathy could well understand, however, the terrible guilt her mother had felt on the death of the husband she had loved so much. Reluctantly she conceded that Randolph had kept his part of the bargain—he must have held her mother very dear to have kept quiet all these years.

She thought of the gentle and tender way Will had revealed the story to her. It couldn't have been an easy thing to do. It struck her that his manner had changed towards her. Gone was the jokey, flirty attitude. It was almost as if—she hardly dared think the word—he truly *cared* for her. And where there was caring, couldn't commitment and love follow?

She scowled at herself in the mirror. She was falling into the trap again, wasn't she? Allowing herself to hope that this gorgeous man might love her when she knew a relationship was out of the question with a Curtis!

CHAPTER NINE

WILL leafed through the latest *Drugs and Therapeutics Bulletin*, his eyes travelling over an article on 'Inhaled Corticosteroids: Management of Patients with Asthma', and the print danced up and down before his eyes. Dammit! How the hell could he concentrate when his mind was constantly wondering whether he'd done the right thing to tell Kathy about Randolph and her mother?

He grinned to himself. He'd asked his uncle such a simple question. 'Why does Kathy Macdowell think you hurt her mother many years ago?' He had never expected such a bombshell!

He and Randolph had been sitting out on the terrace of his uncle's large house, having a drink, one warm evening. The old fellow had still looked peaky after his operation, and Will had put the question to him rather diffidently. They had actually been talking about the Macdowell girls. Randolph had been enthusing about Lindy's riding skills, so it had seemed fairly natural to slip in his question about Lindy's mother.

He recalled the stunned silence that had followed. For a moment he'd thought Randolph hadn't heard him. He'd looked at his uncle and been shocked at the incredibly sad expression that had crossed the man's ashen face.

He'd put a hand on the man's arm. 'I'm sorry, Randolph, I seem to have upset you. Don't answer that—it's nothing to do with me really. It's just that

Kathy seems to have a down on you because of it, and I couldn't believe you would hurt anybody intentionally.'

Randolph Curtis had looked sharply at his nephew. 'She can't possibly know what went on between her mother and me—nobody in the world knows that!'

'Well, then, Uncle, it's your business—you must keep it to yourself. Kathy will have to think what she likes!'

Randolph took a large gulp of whisky and said slowly, 'It happened a long time ago, and I've been thinking for a while that perhaps the truth should be told now. Frankly, the operation gave me a fright—made me realise my own mortality, I suppose. I think it's time the Macdowell girls knew everything—especially,' he added, with a shrewd look at Will, 'as history may be repeating itself!'

Will frowned. 'I don't get it. What truth? What repetition of history?'

The elderly man smiled ruefully. 'I mean that the Macdowell women seem to have a fatal attraction for the Curtises. You see, I loved Rachel Macdowell passionately for some time when her husband was so ill—and I have a feeling that you are now falling for her daughter!'

And then it all came out. How Rachel had turned to Randolph for advice when her husband had become ill, and gradually they had become more attracted to each other. Then she'd discovered she was pregnant a few months before her husband had died. It had only been later, when the baby had arrived, that she'd felt unbearably guilty, unable to continue seeing Randolph.

The old man sighed. 'I know she loved me, but such was her guilt that I eventually promised never to see her again or even help her financially. I've been lonely ever since,' he added simply and sadly. 'And longing to tell my darling Lindy that she's my daughter and, to all intents and purposes, Kathy is my stepdaughter!'

Will was staggered at the discourse. He'd thought he'd known Randolph so well. All he did know was that Randolph's bluff, gruff exterior hid an affectionate heart of gold. Hadn't he, Will, had personal experience of that? He hoped that by telling Kathy about Randolph and Lindy she would realise it, too.

His thoughts came back to the present, and he pulled a photograph out of his breast pocket and studied it for a moment. Kathy's face, framed by a large sunhat and lavish honey-coloured hair, laughed out at him from the picture. It had been taken on board the barge—that fatal afternoon when he'd realised just how many hurdles he had to jump where Kathy and her assumptions about his family were concerned!

Sighing, he pushed the drugs bulletin away, and pulled a brochure towards him containing particulars of John Macdowell's farm. Perhaps he was a fool after all to go ahead with a lease—his future was pretty unpredictable at the moment. And, anyway, if Kathy didn't play a part in that future, how could he stay here? She might wish nothing more to do with the Curtis family when further revelations were revealed and the background behind the land deal came out.

In a week things would be clearer, regarding his father's—and his own—future. Until then he would make no plans. Slowly he tore up the brochure and dropped it in the waste-paper basket.

Kathy looked with troubled eyes at Lindy, who was sitting at the kitchen table and mixing up a mysterious mixture of carrots, spinach and pasta for her vegetarian lunch. Just how and when was she supposed to broach the delicate subject of Lindy's paternity, and, more importantly, how would Lindy take the news—with horror, scepticism or joy?

Kathy took a deep breath and cleared her throat, as if about to jump over a hurdle. Lindy looked up enquiringly.

'Something up? You've been like a cat on hot bricks for days—spit it out! Are you worrying about the dress rehearsal of the play tonight?'

'Er…no, not really,' said Kathy weakly, and started ironing a blouse very vigorously. It wasn't the kind of news one could just spit out, she thought ruefully. No doubt about it, Will had left her with a difficult situation, to say the least!

Lindy started to shred some cheese onto her mixture. 'Thought I'd go up to the stables this afternoon,' she said. 'Randolph's got a new horse, and he said I could go and see it. Might cheer me up after that horrible exam I had this morning.'

Kathy's mouth went dry. 'I thought you had an exam tomorrow as well—what about revision?' she said.

Lindy shrugged carelessly. 'Oh, it'll be easy tomorrow—not like this morning's maths. It was completely impossible, Kathy. I don't think they should torture us with stuff we've hardly done. I could kill that Mrs Brady. She barely finished the syllabus with us—how can I ever be a vet if I don't get maths?'

She looked piteously at Kathy. 'I'll be taking this horrible exam till I'm an old lady,' she grumbled. 'Sarah Philips has a father who's brilliant at maths, so he's helped her all the time. By the way, can I go with them to London for a few days when the exams finish?'

'Of course you can. Sounds like fun…' Kathy's heart constricted with anguish for Lindy. If only she knew that she, too, had a father, who was probably only too willing to help her with her maths, take her on outings… But she couldn't bring herself to tell Lindy yet.

Abstractedly, she finished ironing another blouse, then picked up the local paper and cast a cursory eye over it. Suddenly, with a jolt of consternation, huge black headlines seemed to leap out of the page and scream out at her. FINAL ENQUIRY SANCTIONS LAND SELL-OFF!

So it *was* going to happen. Nothing could now stop the place becoming a holiday leisure centre! For so long she'd hoped and prayed that permission would be refused, or at the very least Randolph Curtis would be persuaded to change his mind.

Furiously, she flung the paper down on the table and looked at Lindy.

'It looks as if we've reached the end of the line with the sale of Randolph's land,' she said tersely. 'Look at that!'

She thrust the paper under Lindy's nose. 'All those petitions and the money we've raised—we might as well have saved our energy!'

Lindy peered at the article and frowned. 'It's funny, you know, but I get the feeling Randolph doesn't want to sell the land really. He's never said anything, but I think he'd be sorry to see it go. Perhaps it's not too late—you'll be seeing Will at the dress rehearsal tonight, won't you? Can't you have another word with him?'

Kathy sighed ruefully. 'Every time I get on to that

subject, we seem to come to blows—but I'll have a go.'

Perhaps, she reflected, the fact that Lindy was against it, too, might sway Randolph to have a last-minute change of heart.

'Never mind, folks! They always say a bad dress rehearsal means that the first night will go well...'

The producer, Molly, looked brightly round at the exhausted cast, and they gave mirthless laughs at her optimistic statement. Everything at the dress rehearsal seemed to have gone wrong, from forgotten lines to bungled entrances and ill-fitting costumes. At that moment, one of the cast was trying to calm an hysterical outburst from a temperamental woman who was saying she was too nervous to go on!

I know how she feels, reflected Kathy wryly. She loved amateur dramatics, but she was beginning to feel there was enough drama to cope with in her own life at the moment.

She glanced over to where Will was helping a group of men move a huge piece of scenery from one side of the stage to the other. When they had finished she was determined to tackle him for the last time about the sale of the land. After all, permission had been given, but it wasn't a *fait accompli*.

He looked up when Kathy came over. His face seemed drawn and desperately tired, but his expression brightened at her approach.

'Hello, there—ready for the big night tomorrow?'

Kathy shuddered. 'I daren't think about it—so many things went wrong tonight I just have to hope it can only get better!'

He waited for a second, then said quietly, 'Have you managed to speak to Lindy yet?'

'No... I can't risk upsetting her at exam time, but I will tell her in the next few days. Quite honestly, I think it'll be the most difficult thing I've ever done, but I know you're right—she needs to know the truth.'

Will nodded. 'I'm glad you see it that way—it could be a happy revelation, you know. I think Lindy is fond of the old boy, and he adores her—I know that.'

Kathy stepped forward eagerly. 'Perhaps that might make him change his mind, then, about the land... I've just seen in the paper that permission has been given for the sale as a holiday complex.'

She saw Will's expression flinch and darken, but charged on eagerly before he could interrupt. 'It's not too late. If Randolph knew how much Lindy is against it, and he loves her, surely he would do what his daughter wants?'

Will was silent, staring at the floor for a moment. Then he looked up and sighed. 'I can't help you there, Kathy. As I've told you before, there really is no way I can influence my uncle, even if I wanted to. The subject is closed, I'm afraid. All I will say is that his reasons for letting it go are unavoidable.'

Kathy almost stamped her foot with frustration. 'This is ridiculous,' she blurted out angrily. 'Why can't you tell me the reason? Then I might understand!'

He shrugged helplessly. 'I can't do that. I'm sorry. I've promised to keep a confidence, and I could never break that promise.' He looked at her, his face stricken. 'Kathy, believe me, I would if...if things were different.'

Kathy flushed. His regard for her couldn't be all that high if he couldn't even tell her *why* Randolph was selling the wretched land. If he could tell her the truth about his uncle, why be so mysterious about this subject?

That was it, then—all over bar the shouting.

'Right. I'll say goodnight!'

Her voice was unnaturally light and dismissive, but there was a huge lump in her throat. She felt as if she'd lost a battle. She turned briskly away from Will and walked out of the hall. She'd tried, she'd done her best, but she would just have to let it go. However, she was bitterly disappointed and, yes, there was a stinging hurt inside her. If Will did care for her at all, there would be no secrets. Surely he would trust her enough to reveal just what it was that made the land sale inevitable.

There was the sound of running footsteps behind her, and she felt her arm caught in a vice-like grip. She was spun round, none too gently. Will's cobalt eyes held hers with a pleading look.

'Kathy, wait for a minute. For God's sake, don't storm off again. Give me a chance to explain...'

'Explain! I keep asking you to, but I get stonewalled. You don't think it matters to me, but it does,' she said passionately. 'Don't you see? If I knew *why* the land was being sold, I might find it easier to understand.'

Will raised his hands in despair then let them drop to his sides. 'I've told you before, I admire your tenacity in fighting for something you believe in but, please, don't let it come between us—that would be so ridiculous.'

He looked down at her with a rather forlorn expression, and Kathy felt a sudden temptation to put her arms around him and hold him close to her. The longing was so great she could almost feel his hard, lean frame against her soft body, the touch of his cheek against hers... Then people began to stream out of the little theatre, jostling and chattering. There was no point in prolonging this discussion in front of them, and Kathy gave a little shrug of hopelessness, nodded a farewell to Will and walked off rapidly down the road.

The afternoon visits the next day went on longer than Kathy had expected as she was delayed, visiting a new-born baby. Alison Brown lived at the furthest end of town, in a flat at the top of four flights of dingy stairs with no working lift. Once Kathy reached the flat, she discovered with irritation that her sphygmomanometer was on the front seat of her car so she had to pound all the way down the stairs and up again. She wondered how Alison was going to manage with a baby and all the paraphernalia a baby needed!

Alison and her partner, Eddy, were both eighteen, and on the face of it things looked rather desperate. But Eddy had just secured a job he loved in the local park and, amazingly, in such a gloomy place, they were cheerful and optimistic.

'Oh, yes, Doctor,' he said chirpily. 'I'll soon have this place to rights. Just needs a lick of paint, doesn't it, darlin'? We were lucky to get it, you know, otherwise we'd have had to live with her parents.'

Kathy reflected that perhaps he was right. Alison's large family lived in cheerful chaos in a tiny house—at least they had this place to themselves!

Alison grinned, childlike in a skimpy cotton dress, holding the tiny baby like a doll in her arms. She looked far too slight to have managed to nurture a child inside her and give birth.

'Social Services are getting us some curtains soon,' she said happily, 'and me sister's given me a carrycot.'

Kathy looked doubtfully round at the peeling walls and cracked sink in the corner. It didn't look the right place to house a newborn baby.

'I'm sure you'll do wonders, Eddy.' She smiled. 'But I'm going to have a word with the housing department and ask if there isn't a flat in better condition. Alison's not very strong at the moment, and she's still slightly anaemic. If we could get you something on the ground floor you wouldn't have to struggle upstairs so much with all the things for little Natasha.'

Eddy said stoutly, 'If we weathered the birth, we can get through anything.' He gave a hoarse chuckle. 'I was more scared when Natasha was born than Alison was, never mind going to those ante-whatsit classes. I passed right out at the birth, and they had to stretcher me away!'

Alison looked at him proudly. 'He's been great. He found an old pram on the tip and he's mending it for me...' Her expression changed slightly and a frown creased her tired young face. 'Actually, Doctor, I wanted to ask you something. Me neighbour came in today and said she could tell the baby was jaundiced 'cos she's a bit yellowish. I've been that worried. Does it mean there's something up with her liver?'

Kathy smiled reassuringly and held out her arms for the infant, cradling her gently in her arms. The baby had the slightly tanned look of a newborn whose immature liver wasn't yet excreting the pigment bilirubin efficiently.

'Don't worry, Alison. She's got something thousands of newborn babies have—a hint of physiological jaundice. The midwife will keep a close watch on it, and in two days I'm sure it will have disappeared. If it hasn't gone after ten days, we'll do a blood test. I'm sure it's just because her system is a little immature.'

The baby had been rather small at birth, and although the midwife would be in daily to check on the child Kathy liked to make sure she saw all the newborns and their mothers as soon as she could. She was glad to reassure Alison.

'She's perfect, Alison. Her umbilical cord's very clean and healing nicely, and all her reactions are fine. Are you getting any sleep at the moment?' She looked at Alison's pale face and the large, dark circles under her eyes.

'Not much,' admitted Alison, 'but I'll live.'

Kathy handed Natasha back to her mother with a lingering look at the tiny form, now flailing her little arms and opening her small mouth wide in a yawn. There was something far too appealing about babies, she thought wistfully. They brought on broody thoughts that she'd rather not have had at the moment!

'Make sure you bring Natasha in for her inoculations and, of course, you need to come in for your postnatal check-up in six weeks, but if you're worried about anything, get in touch with the surgery or tell your midwife.'

Eddy gave her a perky salute. 'Aye, aye, Doc.' He grinned.

It was quite late when she got back to the surgery to write a quick report on Alison and her new baby, and catch up on paperwork. She would also write an urgent letter to the housing department to explain that the conditions Eddy and Alison were living in were totally unsuitable, and asking that some action be taken.

She shot a look at her watch. In a few hours she was going to have to appear on stage, and she felt a leap of fright. Thank God it was only a three-night run! Not for the first time, she wondered why in heaven's name she'd volunteered to take a part. The whole experience was so hair-raising and she was sure she wouldn't remember a single line. Crossly she remembered that it was to help raise money for the land sale protest!

Feeling rather like someone going to the guillotine, Kathy pushed her reports into the drawer of her desk and switched off her computer.

Despite the standard of the dress rehearsal, the play's first night went amazingly well, although the prompter lost her place in the second act and left the cast floundering rather desperately for a few pages. The audience also coped well with a piece of scenery falling heavily during the hero's major speech and the lights failing during the last scene.

Kathy flopped down on an old sofa in the dressing room after the play ended, feeling an overwhelming sense of relief that they'd got through it without a major disaster occurring. She felt quite a high, in fact, the adrenalin of success sweeping through her. Having felt earlier in the day that she'd never have the strength to get through the party that was always held after the first night, she flicked a look towards Will and suddenly felt full of energy.

Everyone seemed exhilarated and rushed round congratulating each other, already swigging back tins of lager in large quantities. Kathy went behind the make-shift curtain that acted as a screen for changing and looked doubtfully at the outfit she was going to change into. Having had little time between surgery and coming to the theatre, she'd just grabbed something she'd thought would be casual and comfortable. As a consequence, instead of the rather prim top and black trousers she'd thought she'd brought, she found she had thrown into her bag a cream silk blouse with rather a low neckline and a pair of tight, black pedal-pushers which she'd forgotten fitted her slightly too snugly!

Then she shrugged. It was too late to rush home now and find something more discreet—she'd just have to hope that her visits to the gym had given her body a firmer profile! She peeped through the curtain, her heart fluttering when she saw Will sitting on the stage at the edge of the wings, looking rather too fabulous for comfort—a white shirt, open at the neck, worn loosely over old jeans. He looked rangy, relaxed and terribly sexy!

Kathy cast a nervous look at her image in the dusty mirror—for some reason a suppressed excitement was building up inside her. Probably relief over getting through the first night, and—dammit—the knowledge that whatever her thoughts about an involvement with Will, she still wanted to be near him, see him, talk to him, and she had that chance tonight!

Someone had put on some loud music with a heavy beat that demanded to be danced to. Peter, her leading man, who fancied himself on the dance floor, came over and persuaded her to dance with him. It was fun. Kathy enjoyed being twirled round the room, and soon the whole cast was joining in—except for Will, she noticed, looking quickly in his direction. He was watching them all with a grin of appreciation and quietly downing a pint. Self-consciously, she realised that her hair had descended from the clips that held it back and was now flying madly round her head and her skimpy blouse had ridden up, showing a large expanse of abdomen, and probably more, she thought with a giggle to herself.

The evening wore on, with no shortage of partners for Kathy, although Will continued to sit stubbornly at the edge of the stage, just watching the proceedings. Peter had staggered off the dance floor earlier for another injection of lager, and Kathy had made inroads on the rather nasty cheap wine on offer. Eventually she sank down, exhausted, on a bench at the side of the room, and suddenly the music changed to the pulsating romance of Elvis Presley, and 'It's Now or Never' throbbed from the speakers.

'Can I persuade you to have the next one with me, Dr Macdowell?' A strong hand took hers and hauled her to her feet.

Kathy looked up at Will's rangy figure, and swallowed hard. Persuade her? Hadn't it been what she had longed for subconsciously all evening? She'd been beginning to think he'd never ask her! She slipped into his arms and he pulled her towards him firmly as they swayed to Elvis.

He held her without speaking for some time. Someone had dimmed the lights and all Kathy could see was his strong profile above her—but she could feel him, feel his body hard and muscular against hers, and, much to her amused surprise, how aroused he was! There was a dreamy, unrealistic atmosphere, heightened by the throbbing music and the relaxed mood of the evening that seemed to relax all inhibitions.

Kathy allowed herself to lean against Will, losing herself in the romance of the moment. She didn't care that he was a Curtis or that she didn't want to get bound up with him—she only knew that this was heavenly. Heavenly to be pressed against the hard wall of his chest, feel his breath on her cheek, smell his male smell.

'Can I ask you something?' he murmured after a while, holding her yet more tightly. 'Are you enjoying this?'

Kathy laughed. 'Doesn't it seem like it? Why do you ask?'

'Perhaps I don't want to do anything you don't want. After all,' he murmured, 'we've been in a similar scene to this before, haven't we?'

'Perhaps,' she suggested roguishly, the wine suddenly beginning to kick in on an empty stomach, 'we could just enjoy it for tonight…'

She snuggled up to him more closely, and then both his arms were round her waist and they were swaying together as if they were one. Gently she pulled his head down to hers. His lips touched hers softly at first, then passionately and fiercely, teased them apart—and at the back of her mind she thought, Tonight I don't care that he's a Curtis. I love this and I'm going to live for the moment!

'Oh, Kathy,' he murmured, nuzzling his face into her neck, 'you are quite the most beautiful heroine here tonight—and I'm finding it very hard to resist you.'

His arms tightened further around her and Kathy gasped. In her slightly heady state she was finding it difficult to resist him as well!

The music stopped and the lights came up gradually, revealing rather bleary-eyed couples disentangling themselves from each other or remaining locked together in oblivion. Will shifted himself slightly away from Kathy, still maintaining his hold around her.

'You left very suddenly last night,' he murmured. 'I thought perhaps you wanted nothing more to do with me. You seemed very cross with me.'

Kathy smiled languorously at him. 'I'm not cross now,' she assured him. She twisted in his arms slightly. 'It's such a stupid thing to do, though, isn't it?'

'What is?'

'Selling the land, of course. It'll never be the same again round here. Why does your uncle have to do it? You're such a secretive family—how can anyone get near a family like yours?'

It was as if she'd pressed a button. She felt his mood change and tense, his relaxed manner fizzling away. His eyes glittered in the low light.

'Can't you *ever* get that bloody subject out of your mind—or the fact that I'm a Curtis?' he said in a dangerously quiet voice.

She looked at him, slightly nonplussed. 'What on earth's the matter? You know how I feel about it.'

He smiled sardonically. 'I know you can take nothing on trust. Good God, just now I was sure there was a magical spark between us, Kathy. I could have sworn that you were enjoying…being together as much as I was. But even in this atmosphere, it always comes back to the same thing with you.'

There was a bitter edge to his voice and Kathy shrugged her shoulders dismissively.

'I can't help feeling passionately about it. You can't possibly understand—'

'Oh, but I think I'm beginning to understand, Kathy. At last the penny's started to drop. Any encouragement you have given me romantically was just so that I would do what you wanted, wasn't it? Oh, yeah, you responded all right, but it was a calculated response—

just enough to persuade me to get the land deal revoked!'

Kathy stared at him, astounded.

'That's just not true!' she gasped.

He looked down at her with a mixture of sadness and resignation in his eyes. 'Well, my dear, I give up. I did hope that perhaps we had something going between us, but every time I think we're getting somewhere the land deal comes up to haunt me. I think I'll have to close this particular chapter of my life. I can't go on defending my family to you any more, or hoping that you're attracted to me for myself alone.'

'What do you mean?' she whispered, the blood draining from her face.

'I mean I've come to the conclusion that I can't really work with you any more, knowing that all you're concerned with is my influence with my uncle. I had hoped that this evening would be different, would perhaps nurture that spark we had into something more. But I was wrong—you're obsessed with one thing, and it isn't me!'

'You've got the whole situation twisted—that's not how it is at all,' protested Kathy hotly.

'I don't think so. I'm handing in my notice now because I don't think we have a future professionally— or any other way. Perhaps I'll go back to Africa where I'm wanted. I'll arrange for a locum to take my place for the time being.'

He gave a little mock bow, and said sadly, 'Goodnight, Kathy.'

He'd strode away before she could say anything else.

CHAPTER TEN

'THAT drug rep's here to see you,' said Ruth, her face appearing round the door like the disembodied Cheshire cat. 'I told him you were busy, but he said he'd made an appointment with the practice. He's very persistent.'

Kathy sighed crossly. She supposed Will had made the appointment and now, of course, he wasn't available. She peeped through the half-open door and saw a very young man clutching a briefcase and a large parcel with BENTHAM DELI written on the side. Most of the reps brought lunch to the doctors nowadays—long, expensive, boozy lunch-hours were out. Kathy guessed that deli food would be the reward he was offering her in exchange for listening to him talk about his product for ten minutes!

She didn't feel like listening to anyone talk for ten seconds, let alone ten minutes. She hadn't got over the shock of Will walking out on her. How had it all gone so wrong so horribly quickly? One minute they were clasped in each other's arms in a passionate embrace, and the next minute he was accusing her of leading him on just to get her own way! A week later she was still bewildered and filled with heart-wrenching regret that she'd jumped to so many wrong conclusions.

Just how stupid could a girl get? Kathy asked herself as she marched to the door and called the young rep into her room. No wonder Will couldn't wait to shake the dust from his shoes and probably head back to

Africa—hadn't she driven him to it with her over-the-top nagging about the land deal? It was too late now to realise that she loved him—and didn't care whether he *was* related to Randolph Curtis or not. It was Will she loved, completely and unreservedly.

If she thought about it too much, she felt a choking sadness that threatened to overwhelm her. That's why she didn't let even a single picture of Will float into her mind. She would just have to manage, as she had before she'd met him. Anything there'd been between them was over, wasn't it?

As she told herself repeatedly, she could cope perfectly well without Will Curtis in her life. She had no need of him at all... Surely she wasn't the feeble type of woman who was lost without a man?

Kathy realised suddenly that the young man was now standing in the middle of the room, staring at her rather uncomfortably, not too sure whether to sit down or not. He looked very young and vulnerable. She'd certainly never seen him before, and guessed that perhaps this was his first job.

'Er, sorry—do sit down.' Kathy forced a faint smile to make him feel at ease. 'Perhaps you'd like to start telling me straight away about this acid inhibitor?'

Her voice came out more tersely than she'd intended, and the young man looked slightly alarmed.

'You...you wouldn't like some lunch first?' he asked hesitatingly.

Kathy smiled grimly to herself. Obviously he'd been told this was a good ploy to soften up the uncooperative customer—food first, spiel later! She almost felt sorry for him—she was going to be a very hard nut to crack in her present mood!

He looked at her expression and said hastily, 'Perhaps I'll give you the gen on our new proton pump inhibitor now—very effective in cases of intractable stomach ulcers...'

The rep's voice droned on and Kathy's thoughts turned inwards again. It had taken nearly twenty-nine years for her to meet the love of her life—and she'd tossed him away as carelessly as if one came across that sort of star every year... By the time she met another suitable candidate she'd probably be nearly sixty! She couldn't really believe the comforting saying that there were plenty more fish in the sea.

She sighed heavily, and the young man looked at her nervously.

'It's all right,' she informed him brusquely. 'Just clearing my throat. It sounds an interesting product— I'll think about it.'

'Won't...won't you have some salmon mousse now?' The young man tentatively pushed some food towards Kathy. 'It's very good...'

'Sorry, don't feel terribly hungry today.' Kathy's heart melted somewhat at the rep's crestfallen expression. He obviously thought that if he couldn't even get rid of the free lunch he'd brought, he certainly wouldn't be able to offload his acid inhibitor!

'Take it through to Reception,' she told him more gently. 'I'm sure Ruth and our practice nurse are hungry!'

Will was still around—Kathy could see his little car parked in its familiar place. He was coming in occasionally to ease the way for the locum, an older man who'd taken early retirement from his practice. Bill Burton was very pleasant, but he wasn't Will! She felt none of the eager anticipation at the start of the day

when she came to the centre, just a dull ache, com-
pounded by the fact that it was all her fault that things
had gone so drastically wrong between them.

The flowers in the little bed by the side of the surgery car park had matured into a very pretty herbaceous
border, and a neatly painted new sign by the gate pro-
claimed that it was indeed the Bentham Medical
Centre. Already the builders had started the new ex-
tension at the side of the building. Soon it would bear
no resemblance to the dilapidated structure that had
been there when Will had first arrived. In a few weeks
the place had been transformed. Oh, yes, Will Curtis
had left his mark on many things...

Kathy pushed herself impatiently away from her
desk. Positive thought, she instructed herself firmly.
She'd had enough of brooding over Will. Today was
the first day of her new life—off with the old, on with
the new! It was her free afternoon and she was going
to do something she'd been meaning to do for some
time...

Strands was a hairdresser's in Bentham High Street,
staffed by men and girls with impossibly slim figures
and beautifully streaked and extended hair. Kathy
didn't use the hairdresser's much, but when she did she
always felt extra large and slightly out of date.

She glanced at herself in one of the wall-to-wall mir-
rors. The brilliant lighting seemed to highlight how
dowdy she felt beside the rest of the staff and clientele.
Kathy winced. After she'd finished here she was going
to blow a horrible amount of money on a dark cinna-
mon-coloured trouser suit she'd seen in a local bou-
tique, and a pair of ruinously expensive boots!

An anorexic-looking girl with a pre-Raphaelite mane

of red hair and black lipstick took Kathy's sensible jacket and whipped a white cape over her shoulders.

'Bernard will attend to you in a moment,' she breathed.

Bernard always went into ecstasies over Kathy's hair's thickness and natural colour. He hailed her like a long-lost friend.

'Dr Macdowell! What a pleasure to see you! Just the usual dry trim?' He held up a strand of hair disapprovingly. 'I see we've let our hair get a little dry—a few split ends here and there. You could do with a treatment.'

Kathy looked at him with a defiant air. 'Then give me the full treatment, Bernard—I need a change of image. I want you to cut the lot off!'

She watched, rather stupefied, as her thick hair tumbled to the ground, and a different, gamin-like version of her face began to appear. Her previous life being stripped away, she thought glumly. What the hell had she done? She had a sudden horrible vision of a tiny head on top of a strapping body and gulped nervously as Bernard's scissors flashed dexterously about her head.

He blow-dried her shortened crop into a bouncy bob round her face, then stepped back, looking at her critically in the mirror with narrowed eyes.

'Excellent!' he pronounced. 'Now you see your beautiful cheekbones—and look how large your eyes seem. You should have done this a long time ago!'

Kathy looked doubtfully at her image—it seemed to give her a more sophisticated, capable look. She straightened her shoulders—great! That's just what she'd wanted to achieve, she told herself firmly. She remembered that Will had told her never to cut her hair.

Well, she could live without him and his advice! It was too late now—new life, here I come!

'Ooh, you look fabulous, Dr Macdowell. I hardly recognised you!'

'Thanks,' said Kathy dryly, then grinned as Ruth clapped a hand to her mouth.

'Sorry, I didn't mean that you looked, well, unattractive before…but this is a real change.'

'Thought I'd go for a new image, Ruth—rather like you.'

Ruth blushed. 'I thought it was time really—had the same hairstyle for too long.'

'Quite right. That's how I felt.' Kathy looked with a sly grin at Ruth. 'And does Charlie Lennox approve?'

She'd realised for some time that the catalyst which had started Ruth's transformation had been Charlie, the builder. She'd watched Ruth and him walking hand in hand from the surgery several times! As she'd surmised before, love had been the motivation for Ruth's change of style—love lost had been Kathy's impetus.

Ruth gave a most uncharacteristic giggle and hurried from the room. Kathy gazed after her almost enviously. At least one romance seemed to be on line!

It had been one of the hardest things Kathy had ever done, to tell Lindy that Randolph Curtis was her father. She'd decided that her new, tougher image would give her the confidence to break the news, and after a glass of red wine to give her Dutch courage she had finally burst into her surprised sister's room.

The reality of telling Lindy had been easier than she'd thought, and her sister's reactions, although bewildered at first, became one almost of excitement mixed with disbelief.

'Let me go and see him and then I might really begin to believe it,' she begged Kathy, then she looked at her sister's face. 'It…it must be difficult for you, Kath. I know you're not too keen on him, but I've always quite liked him, you know. And…' She looked at the older girl with wide eyes. 'This makes me Will Curtis's cousin—isn't that *great*?'

'Great,' said Kathy hollowly, thinking how ironic it was that her connection with Will was closer than it had ever been, just as she'd driven him away from her!

She looked at Lindy—bright, bubbly, loving Lindy—and thought how lucky Randolph Curtis was to be reunited with a daughter like her.

'If you want to see him, I think that you should go,' she said gently. 'I'll ring him up to tell him you're on your way, and then I'll drive you up there. I won't stay. I think you'll have a lot to talk about!'

Lindy flung her arms round Kathy and laughed happily. 'It's a peculiar feeling, knowing I've got a father—but you're my sister first and foremost!'

The house seemed cold and cheerless. Rafter lay asleep contentedly in front of the small fire Kathy had lit, taking all the heat there was and giving little sighs and yelps as he dreamt of chasing rabbits.

'You're the only one that needs me now, Rafter,' said Kathy sadly to him. He wagged his tail gently at the mention of his name, his eyes still shut. 'I seem to have made a pig's ear of my life so far, don't I?'

Rafter wagged his tail again, agreeing with her.

'It was a mistake to let Will Curtis join the practice, wasn't it?' she said dispiritedly. Rafter snored.

Depressed, Kathy switched on the television. Perhaps there'd be a sparkling, humorous sitcom on to take her mind off the grim reality of being alone and unloved. However, it turned out to be the local news. A woman was talking earnestly about crime in the area, a local chef had won a national cookery competition— and suddenly Kathy's eyes widened in astonishment and she almost stopped breathing! Unbelievably, Will's face, smiling broadly, swam into view on the screen!

She gasped. What the hell was he doing in front of the Crown Court Building, with crowds of people round him and his arm supporting an elderly man by his side?

She leaned forward till her nose was almost touching the screen, and turned the sound up loudly.

Will's deep voice boomed across the room. 'I would just like to thank the people who have supported my father in his quest for justice. We always knew he was innocent, and now that he has finally been proved so on this appeal he can get back to living his life and looking forward to the future.'

His face faded from the screen and an announcer questioned a solicitor who said that new evidence had come to light, proving irrefutably that Gordon Curtis had played no part in the charge of embezzlement from the law firm in which he was a partner.

Kathy gave a shriek of surprise, causing Rafter to jump. He woke up and gave her a reproachful look as he shook himself and sloped off to the kitchen.

'I can't believe it!' she whispered to herself. 'Will's father was in prison!'

Why hadn't he told her? Surely he must have known she wouldn't have thought the worst of him? Then she remembered how Will had talked of giving a promise not to reveal anything and recalled his obvious reluctance to speak of his father. Some things began to fall slowly into place—his cryptic comments about his father, and how his father would love the space of her cousin's farm after the place he was in at the moment.

Another soothing glass of wine and a hot bath seemed to be in order whilst she digested this astounding news. Kathy had known Will had come back to support his father. She had thought it had been because his father had been ill. She would never have guessed in a million years that Gordon Curtis had been in prison! Now, she thought bleakly, Will had even less reason to stay here as his father had won his case.

Kathy shrugged her body farther under the comforting hot soapy water of the bath, and regarded her toes morosely. Perhaps she'd take up cross-country running, or golf, or even bridge—anything that didn't remind her of periwinkle blue eyes set in a tanned, strong face. Tomorrow she'd make a list of things to aim for, to get good at. She stepped out of the bath briskly and threw on a silk shortie nightie.

What else was there to do at the moment but go to bed? Lindy had rung earlier to say she was staying the night with Randolph. She had sounded full of suppressed excitement—Kathy wondered if he had told her about Will's father. Lindy had gabbled down the phone that she had so much to tell Kathy tomorrow, and there were so many plans to be made. Kathy hadn't been able to get a word in edgeways! She snapped the light off beside her bed and lay, as tense as a board, trying to sleep.

She must have eventually dozed off, because the sound of hammering seemed to coincide with a dream she was having of the roof being mended at the practice. Gradually she was aware that it was her own front door that was being attacked.

She sat bolt upright—what the hell was happening? Various thoughts raced through her head, including the alarming idea that Gary Layton had come back to get his revenge on her! She slipped out of bed, grabbing an old cardigan from a chair and wrapping it closely around her. She seized a tennis racket, propped up against the wall in the hall, and held it menacingly in the air, shouting through the door before she opened it.

'What do you want—and who is it?'

'Who do you *think* it is?' The voice was familiar, deep and impatient.

Kathy opened the door gingerly, her racket poised above her head.

Blue eyes swept over her, and a smile twitched on firm lips.

'What the hell have you done to your hair?' asked Will.

Kathy stared at him, completely bewildered, her heart hammering at the sudden and unexpected proximity of his absurdly handsome presence. Was she still dreaming? She'd seen him on television only an hour or two previously. She put a protective hand up to her head.

'I had it cut,' she said unnecessarily. Then, pulling herself together and clutching her ridiculously short cardigan inadequately around herself in some semblance of dignity, she remarked coldly, 'I saw you on the news. I thought you'd be at your uncle's, celebrating. What on earth have you come round for?'

'Perhaps you'd better let me in. I can tell you why I've come then, and it may prevent you contracting double pneumonia on the doorstep, dressed in that, er, delightfully scanty outfit you're wearing.'

Kathy stepped back obediently, her mind whirring like an overwound clock. 'I didn't know your father was in prison. You kept that very secret,' she said, faint accusation in her voice. 'Didn't you think I'd understand if you told me? So much would have been clearer to me if I'd known.'

'I *told* you, I gave my word. My father didn't want me to tell anyone—except my uncle, of course. And that's partly why I've come.'

'What more is there to tell?' asked Kathy, a mite wearily. So, his father was out of prison. She was pleased for him, but it was nothing to do with her now, was it?

Will caught her hand urgently. 'As I said, part of my reason for coming was to do with my father's release. You see, now that he's been found innocent we don't have to find any money—the case has been won. Randolph was going to sell the land to raise the cash, and now he doesn't have to!'

He watched her face as she stared at him. 'You mean,' she said falteringly at last, 'that was the reason he was selling it—to provide funds for your father's appeal?'

He nodded. 'He never wanted to sell it really, but we were desperate and it seemed the only way. So you see, now you have something to celebrate as well— and perhaps, just perhaps, it shows that Randolph isn't the shark you thought he was.'

Kathy turned from him and looked at his reflection in the little living-room mirror. 'It is great news,' she said quietly. 'I'm delighted.' She wheeled towards him.

'Thanks for coming to tell me personally although, no doubt, I would have heard about it eventually.'

'I told you that was only part of my reason for coming here.'

'What else is there, then?' Kathy felt empty, drained. It was nice of him to come and tell her the momentous news about the sale, but for some curious reason she felt no lift in spirits—just horribly flat and depressed. She'd driven Will away by her constant harping about Randolph's land, and in the end it hadn't mattered. The countryside would stay the same—but her life had changed for ever.

He shrugged. 'I thought you'd guess, you funny little shorn lamb. I have some unfinished business with you, Kathy Macdowell.'

Kathy looked blankly at him. 'What do you mean? You said all that you had to say very clearly the other night, didn't you?' There was a hint of bitterness in her voice.

He held her at arm's length for a second, his eyes filled with a sort of exasperated tenderness. 'Perhaps I wasn't totally correct after all about your motives. I've had a bit of time to reflect, and I reckon you do like me a little bit, even if I *am* part of the dreaded Curtis family. I don't care if you don't love me yet—you're bound to fall for my many charms sooner or later...'

Astounded, Kathy's heart began to hammer erratically, and a glimmer of bright happiness seemed to beckon from somewhere on the horizon.

'What...what's made you think that?' she said breathlessly.

'Because,' he grinned impishly, 'no girl would respond like you did to someone they didn't like. You're not *that* good an actress! I just can't give up on us,

Kathy. No matter what happened to my father, I began to realise that I just couldn't leave you—I need you too much, my darling.'

He pulled her gently towards him and bent his head to hers, gently brushing his lips against her soft mouth. Somewhere inside her a delirious feeling of rapture began to well up. She was unresistant as his arms slid round her and held her tightly against him, and she leaned against him, delighting in the sensation of his hard body on hers.

His lips trailed down her neck, his hands gently eased off the cardigan and the silky nightie slipped to the floor.

Suddenly Kathy began to realise something very clearly—she'd obviously been wrong. She couldn't do without William Curtis after all!

'What are you doing?' she whispered. She stood very still, her eyes widening, her lips parted languorously.

'What do you think? Doing something I should have done before—telling you I love you body and soul.'

Will's strong hands caressed her naked body softly, as he covered her breasts with butterfly kisses.

'Why didn't you tell me before?' she murmured as his kisses became more urgent. She began to undo his shirt.

'I didn't want to frighten you off…'

'It doesn't frighten me that you love me,' Kathy said softly, pulling off his shirt and laying her head on his bare chest. 'You see, I've loved you from the day I first saw you—although I thought I shouldn't because you were a Curtis!'

'And now?'

She laughed softly. 'Perhaps I don't think the Curtises are so bad after all—especially this one!'

He grinned. 'Then let's start all over again,' he whispered. 'I'm William Curtis MD, and I'd like to get to know you better. But before we go into the bedroom—''

'Who said anything about bedrooms?'

'Here will do, then,' he allowed. 'Let me just make things clear—when are we getting married?'

Kathy's heart did a somersault. 'I thought...' she said breathlessly, 'I thought next week would be all right.'

Will smiled tenderly at her. 'Pencil it in your diary, then, Dr Macdowell. And now,' he said firmly, 'let's make up for lost time, my love.'

He shrugged off the rest of his clothes and carried her into the bedroom.

MILLS & BOON®

Makes any time special™

Mills & Boon publish 29 new titles every month. Select from...

Modern Romance™   Tender Romance™

Sensual Romance™

Medical Romance™   Historical Romance™

MAT2

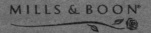